CAPTAIN ENRIQUE BLIGH HORTA 100 TIMES AROUND THE EARTH

BY

Henry Horta

ISBN:
978-1-968973-79-7

TABLE OF CONTENTS

Preface

When I wrote my first book, Adventures and Memoirs of an Airline Pilot, I was living the dream: flying the mighty Boeing 747 across the Pacific, sailing my boat into Hawaiian sunsets, and raising a family on the island paradise of Oahu. Life had its rhythm then: the thrill of the skies, the peace of the ocean, the joy of writing down stories that had accumulated over decades of adventure, mischief, and near-death experiences. I thought that book was a closing chapter.

Turns out it was just the intermission.

Captain BLIGH Flies Again is not just a continuation. It's a reckoning. It's what happens after the dream job collapses, after the airline goes bankrupt, after the surf session ends, and real life throws another storm your way. This book picks up where the last one left off, but it goes deeper. Into war zones disguised as contracts. Into the loneliness of distant hotels. Into friendships forged in cockpits and tensions cracked open by cultural misunderstandings. Into deserts, oceans, and foreign cities where danger and beauty dance side by side.

If my first book was about becoming a pilot, this one is about staying human while being one.

I've flown for 15 airlines in over a dozen countries and lived through UFO sightings, engine failure, and cabin fires. I've surfed forbidden beaches, been mugged in marketplaces, and prayed for my life in freezing Atlantic swells. This isn't just a memoir of places I've been or jets

I've flown. This is a tribute to the unpredictable journey of saying yes to life. Over and over again.

So buckle up, reader. This isn't a manual or a flight log. It's a heart-pounding, salt-crusted, sky-chasing ride. And it's all true.

Captain Enrique Bligh Horta

Chapter 1

The Thunderstorm Landing

Captain Bligh Horta

100 times around the world. Present times.

I seemed to be in a surreal dream.

Heavy rain was striking the windshield of what appeared to be a submerged spacecraft. The cockpit shook violently, as if a giant, unseen monster had its jaws wrapped around the aircraft, trying to crush it from the outside. Thunder cracked like gunfire in the distance, and the roar of the engines blended with the steady scream of the storm outside.

My heart was pounding like a carnival drum. I could feel the adrenaline surging, flooding even the furthest corners of my brain. Every nerve in my body was lit like a live wire.

It wasn't just fear. It wasn't just excitement. It was a mixture of emotion so intense it bordered on the divine, like standing at the edge of life and looking directly into it.

And then, just like that, I snapped back.

Reality hit hard. This wasn't a dream. This was real.

I was at the controls of a Boeing 747, preparing for an approach into Alexandroupolis, a small Greek airport on the eastern edge of the country. My crew, an international mix of aviators, were alert and tense. I had a Latino first officer beside me and two Aussie pilots seated behind us in the observer jumpseats. Everyone was quiet. Focused.

Earlier, the forecast had been promising. Weather well above minimums for a VOR non-precision approach to runway 07. Three miles of visibility. Broken ceiling at 800 feet. Winds gusting to 36 knots from the south. Crosswinds are hitting us hard from the right.

We were carrying eighty-five tons of sensitive "toys" that we'd picked up in Bahrain. Humanitarian aid, they called it. Final destination: Israel. But of course, we couldn't fly it directly. That would break the Arab Brotherhood agreement, an unofficial but strictly observed rule of courtesy and diplomacy.

But that was then.

Now, on approach, the weather had worsened. Cumulonimbus clouds towered around the airfield. Heavy rain battered the aircraft. The visibility we were promised had turned into a wall of moving grey.

"We've got one shot at this," I told my crew flatly. "Otherwise, we divert."

We had an alternate airport on standby, but Alexandroupolis's single 8,400-foot runway, non-grooved but still within Boeing friction specs, was our best option. The weather, though ugly, was still above the minimum. Barely.

As a captain in command, I made the call. We'd try the approach.

"If we have to go around," I briefed, "we request immediate right climbing turn. Avoid that cumulus buildup off the end of the runway."

We descended, configuring early for landing. Everything had to be stabilized by one thousand feet. The runway had to be in sight. And it was.

Mostly.

The strong right crosswind was pushing the plane sideways. The aircraft naturally weathervaned, its nose drifting right, off the centerline. I applied steady rudder and aileron inputs to keep our alignment true. The plane felt stubborn, but it obeyed.

Just as we passed below the cloud base, the runway lights shimmered in the distance. But then the rain intensified, blinding sheets of it.

"Wipers on," I called.

My first officer fumbled overhead. His hand trembled under the sudden jolt of turbulence.

"I can't find the switches!" he shouted, panic rising in his voice.

"I still have the runway," I snapped. "Keep your eyes on your instruments."

I could just make out the centerline lights ahead. My heart was racing. I initiated the flare while stepping on the left rudder to align the aircraft's nose to de-crab it, aligning our longitudinal axis with the runway just before touchdown.

There was no time to float. No margin. The tires met the wet asphalt with a gentle but firm thud.

"The eagle has landed, I muttered as I applied maximum reversers on all engines.

The thrust reversers roared open. Autobrakes set to level four. My feet hovered over the pedals, ready. The aircraft wanted to stop, but it didn't.

Instead, we skidded, hydroplaning. The tires weren't gripping. A thin layer of water on the runway was enough to rob us of traction. It was like sliding a two-hundred-and ninety-ton beast across glass.

"We're not stopping!" my first officer cried out. "It's not stopping!"

I slammed my feet onto the brakes, manual override. Every muscle in my legs strained as I leaned my full weight into the pedals. My eyes locked on the rapidly approaching runway's end. We were running out of time.

Suddenly, the plane began to decelerate. The tires finally caught. The momentum shifted, throwing our bodies forward.

A loud crash behind us.

I didn't look back, but I knew what it was. The galley oven had broken loose from its casing during the rapid deceleration. It slammed against the bulkhead near the cockpit with a dull, metal thud. We came to a full stop.

Two hundred feet. That's how much runway remained beneath us.

I exhaled.

I closed the thrust reversers and slowly began a cautious 180-degree turn to taxi back the opposite way down the runway. My hands were still gripping the yoke tighter than they should. My chest heaved. My nuts felt like they were at my throat.

I turned to my first officer, who sat wide-eyed and pale. "You alright?" I asked.

He gave a slow nod. "I think I need to change my boxers.

I laughed nervously. So did the Aussies in the back. It was the laugh you released when you just barely dodged disaster. We all knew how close it had been.

For a second, I really thought we were going to end up as another episode on Air Crash Investigation, with our wreckage scattered across the Mediterranean coastline, picked apart by satellites and news media.

But no.

Not today.

We were alive. We were intact.

It was a Mommy, I need another diaper moment.

And that, in this business, is always the win.

Moments like this remind me of a saying we have in aviation, one that's more truth than joke:

"Airline flying is described as long moments of boredom, punctuated by sheer moments of terror."

Very true.

Chapter 2

Flying Into the Past

It's now 2024 or 2025, and for those of you who read my first book, I left off living the dream in Hawaii in 2009.

Adventures and Memoirs of an Airline Pilot was the title by Captain Enrique Bligh Horta. If you haven't read it, don't worry. I'll give you a short description of some of those events worth mentioning.

Just a quick recap.

After flying in Mexico for six years for two airlines and a corporate flying job out of Puerto Vallarta with Aerotron, things took an unexpected turn. On my last flight there, we had a full-on inflight fire just after takeoff. (I'll briefly describe it later in this book.) The other two airlines were Aviacsa and Taesa Airlines, both of which eventually went bankrupt by early 1996.

That same year, I landed a short-term but well-paid first officer position with Air New Zealand on the Boeing 767. It was a lovely time, living in Auckland for most of 1996. But by the end of that year, I was hired by Air Mauritius. A beautiful, exotic island, full of new adventures and surprises.

I eventually left Air Mauritius in July 1999 to fly for the previous National Airlines. After three years flying the Boeing 767 there, I literally escaped what I called Mauritius Alcatraz in the middle of the night for various reasons: a severe case of island fever, woman trouble, police trouble, and a death threat. That's not even counting the airline management, who were notorious for broken promises and lying. I won't go into the full details, except to say I took the death threat seriously. I had also run out of aliases after signing speeding tickets as "El Zorro." The cops were on to me.

Plus, I had a better offer from the new 1999 startup, National Airlines out of Las Vegas. Thanks to my good old mate Captain Ross Brightman, they offered me a Captain position on the Boeing 757.

Unfortunately, the fun didn't last. That flying gig only held up until the end of 2002, when National went bankrupt. My oldest teenage son and I, who had been living aboard my sailboat at Harbor Island in San Diego for a couple of years, were now surviving on my savings and credit cards.

Luckily, within a few months, I got a job flying for Japan Airlines, based in Honolulu. Thanks to my sailor neighbor, Ron Dubois, who referred me to the wasinc broker. Eventually, I had to sail my boat to Hawaii, but that's another story and adventure all its own. The journey took 19 days at open sea with no major mishaps. Unlike the first crossing two years earlier, which had nearly ended in disaster.

On that first crossing of the Pacific Ocean, we had a knockdown and almost lost the boat, but we recovered. The owner hadn't heeded my warning about motor sailing with full sails extended at night. We got caught in a squall with strong vertical gusts that knocked the boat onto its side for a few terrifying moments. The boat's stability was recovered thanks to MY quick action releasing the mainsheet line and allowing the weight of the keel to upright us. We narrowly avoided taking on water and sinking in the middle of the Pacific.

We were lucky. Water didn't enter quickly through the aft cockpit. We acted fast. It had started on a quiet night when the skipper's 22-year-old son wanted to race across the Pacific on this 46-foot Hunter with full sails up and motor running.

Bad idea. I warned the owner not to do this at night due to the threat of squalls. He didn't listen. He said not to worry. They knew what they were doing.

Well, they didn't.

We were below, reviewing weather faxes, and Harry the skipper had just stepped down to the bathroom. He left the boat unattended on autopilot. That's when the squall hit us.

Before we knew it, we were knocked down sideways. A full knockdown.

It's the scariest feeling in a pitch black night in the middle of the ocean. Like an invisible hand slams your boat sideways. I knew what to do. Release the mainsheet line. That's the rope attached to the boom on the mainsail. It controls the sail shape and the speed of the boat.

Releasing it would depower the sail before water could pin it down and cause the boat to take on water. That was the only way to prevent water from flooding in and sinking us.

Once I released it, the keel's weight slowly started to upright the boat. I grabbed the helm and tried to face us into the wind because by then we had gone through three accidental jibes due to shifting winds.

An accidental jibe is when the boom, which is the horizontal pole that extends from the mast, swings violently from one side to the other. Sailors have died that way, or been knocked overboard.

Harry had tried to head into the wind but couldn't see the compass clearly. I had to take over.

As I held the heading steady and adjusted to the changing wind, the other two sailors went to the front with tethers and safety lines to cut the remaining ripped-up Genoa sail that was tangled everywhere.

There was damage to the preventer tube and the Genoa head sail, but everything else was fine. The mess inside the boat and our bruised egos were the only other casualties. We survived.

Once the weather passed, we caught our breath over a cold Corona and assessed the damage. Montree finally understood what I'd been warning him about. This time, he took me seriously. He and I agreed: Popeye's son was not to touch the sailboat controls again.

The kid didn't take that very well. He threw a tantrum and stomped below into his cabin, and we didn't see him for nearly two days.

Chapter 3

Lessons on the Wind – The Second Crossing to Hawaii

There's something sacred about a second crossing. It holds the memories of the first, its bruises, its wisdom, its near disasters, and folds them gently into the anticipation of doing it better. That's exactly what I set out to do in the summer of 2004 when I decided to sail my beloved Tequila, a West Sail 42, from San Diego to Honolulu, Hawaii.

Tequila was more than just a boat. She was a companion, a fortress, and a floating piece of history.

Built in Costa Mesa, California, in the mid-70s, her hull was built with a thick hand-laid fiberglass construction, tough enough to take a bullet. With her classic cutter rig, full skeg keel, and barndoor-style rudder, she wasn't built for speed. She was built for the kind of stability that made the ocean feel like home. From bowsprit to stern, she stretched 47 feet of confidence. And unlike those speedy production boats with flimsy keels, like that cursed Hunter 46 that nearly drowned us two years earlier, Tequila was made to dance with the sea, not wrestle it.

By then, I had earned my 50-ton captain's license and logged over a decade on the water. I wasn't green anymore. My previous Pacific crossing had been a rough schooling, one that taught me what to do and, more importantly, what not to do when tackling the vastness of the open sea.

Preparation began months in advance. It wasn't just about fixing the hardware, though there was plenty of that. I overhauled everything from primary rigging to sheets and halyards, updated the electronics with a modern radar system capable of traffic collision avoidance, and installed a new autopilot, GPS, and marine radios. I skipped the satellite phone, thinking it was unnecessary. In hindsight, I'll admit having one would have been a good idea.

There were hours spent in marine stores, poring over gear: a man overboard recovery kit, a sturdy six-man survival raft, a brand-new EPIRB emergency locator beacon. And spares, boxes of them. Belts, fuses, hoses, clamps, anything I could think of that might break. I even taught myself basic celestial navigation, just in case the electronics failed.

One thing I learned the hard way from my first crossing was provisioning. Last time, we'd run out of essentials by day ten. That left us eating fish and rice, breakfast, lunch, and dinner, for the next nine. We joked about it: "What? Not lice again?" we'd say, squinting like cartoon caricatures of ourselves. This time, I packed 30% more supplies, more water, more food, more beer, more wine, and of course, more tequila.

My crew for this journey was a mix of old and new. Harry, affectionately known as "Popeye," was back from our first voyage. His experience and grit made him indispensable. This time, though, his adrenaline-junkie son stayed ashore. Filling the third berth was Boris, my German friend, who had begged to join despite only having lake sailing experience. I warned him: this wasn't some beer-can race on German lakes, this was the Pacific.

We ran and practiced drills before setting out: man-overboard recovery, storm handling tactics, emergency jibing, and tacking. I gathered Harry and Boris in the cockpit on the final day of preparation.

"Out there," I told them, pointing toward the endless blue, "we're all responsible. But make no mistake, I'm the owner and the skipper. Final decisions rest with me."

They both nodded in agreement. At the time, it felt solid.

But once we were underway, the cracks started to show.

Three days in, the alternator began acting up. The batteries wouldn't charge. We were burning precious diesel trying to keep our battery bank charged up. I cursed myself for not installing solar panels or a wind generator. Harry, ever the diesel whisperer, said, "Don't worry, I'll sort it out." True to his word, he did, rigging a secondary circuit bus to keep the alternator charging.

The bigger issue wasn't mechanical. It was Boris. At first, he kept quiet, helping where he could, taking notes like a tourist who'd packed a GoPro and dreams. But when equipment started failing, as it always does at sea, he turned sour.

"This boat is too old," he grumbled one evening while inspecting a winch. "You should've done a better job preparing."

I snapped my head toward him. "You think boats don't break out here? Even brand-new ones? You're lucky Tequila's as tough as she is."

He didn't back down. And neither did I.

By day seven, tensions boiled over.

We were both in the galley when I lost it. "Stop being a damn baby, Boris," I said, stepping closer. "It's too late to call your mommy now."

His jaw tensed. His fists clenched. The air thickened.

Just before fists flew, Popeye stepped between us with the calm of a sea monk, holding two cold Pacificos. "Boys," he said in his gravelly voice, "you done fighting now?"

The way he said it, dry, amused, almost philosophical, cut the tension like a knife. We burst out laughing. The fight fizzled into foam, like a breaking wave.

Later, I sat Boris down for a serious talk. I reminded him of the safety protocols we had practiced: coiled lines, tidy decks, and always clip-in when moving topside. But he and Harry had grown lazy, beer cans, cigarette butts, and unsecured lines cluttered the deck like some floating frat house. It wasn't just sloppy, it was dangerous.

The next day, Boris ignored the rules again. Deciding to sunbathe in nothing but his Speedos on the stern, untethered. A squall was coming. Popeye and I saw it forming on the horizon, dark, curling, angry.

We didn't say a word.

When it hit, it hit hard, rain like nails, wind howling. Boris scrambled like a cat dropped into a tub, slipping and sliding back into the cockpit, screaming, "Scheisse! Where did that come from?"

We couldn't help but laugh. But then I leveled with him again.

"You could've gone overboard, Boris. You're not Poseidon. Wear the damn tether."

From that moment, he shaped up.

The rest of the crossing went by in relative peace. We instated a new rule, no booze after 9 p.m., and I enforced the cleanup of all cans and butts. When they jokingly suggested mutiny one night, I shot them a look that said, "Try me." They didn't. (and this is why they nicknamed me Captain Bligh). The a**hole, strict, and mean captain from the movie "Mutiny on the Bounty".

But none of that could ruin the magic of the journey. There's something spiritual about being in the middle of the Pacific. Just you, your boat, and the breathing rhythm of the sea. The night watches were my favorite moments. I truly enjoyed my three hours of starlight and solitude. The sound of water against the hull. The endless dome of stars above.

Out there, you forget what land feels like. And you remember something older than memory, what it means to trust the wind, your boat, and yourself.

Chapter 4

The Surfari – Morocco, 1984

I felt then as I had once felt in the vast stillness of the Spanish Sahara, now called the French Sahara, during a safari expedition in the winter of 1984. In the endless stretch of desert sand or the raw churn of the ocean, a man becomes something smaller than a grain of salt. You feel insignificant, vulnerable, like a fleeting spark of the cosmos drifting between wind and wave. And yet, in that space, you become part of something eternal.

The Moroccan surfari had already been chronicled in my previous book, but that wild slice of life deserves its echoes here, at least briefly. It was my second backpacking trip through Europe and North Africa, a trip that would leave sun-etched memories I could still feel decades later.

I left Ocean Beach, California, with my new Dutch female friend, Inky, who had convinced me to spend a few days with her family in Holland before heading off on my own. We parted ways shortly after a week at her house. Inky stayed home with her family, and I turned south, hitchhiking my way through the cold belly of winter toward Southern Spain.

The call of Morocco was strong. It was cheap, exotic, and most important of all, teeming with uncrowded waves waiting to be ridden.

From Algeciras, I took the ferry across the Strait of Gibraltar to Tangier. The moment I stepped off the boat, I was hit by the scent of cumin, diesel, and sea salt. The air was brisk and foreign. As I stood near the port with my backpack and my guitar, a rickety surf blue van rolled by, and four French guys leaned out the window, all sun-blonde hair and broad grins.

"Eh, t'es un surfeur?" one of them shouted.

"Yeah, man!" I yelled back.

"You guys heading south?"

One of them opened the sliding door.

"Hop in!"

Later, I found out that the reason they stopped was to inquire where to buy some good hashish. Apparently, I looked like a Moroccan hippy.

And just like that, I joined their crew. Four young French soul surfers with a shared hunger for Atlantic swell and the patience to chase it down Morocco's rugged coast. Their names were Julian, Marc, Didier, and Luc, and they carried with them precious cargo: wetsuits, surfboards of all sizes, and even windsurfing gear. They also had a single-burner stove, fishing rods, and an old cassette player that mostly spat out scratchy Bob Marley and French punk.

For a few weeks, we were our own rolling tribe. We chased waves from Tanger down the coast. Rabat, Casablanca, El Jadida, Safi. Eventually, on the way back, we returned via Marrakech, which was one of the most ancient and beautiful cities I had ever seen.

Along the coastal towns, the air was always laced with salt. We would surf for hours, fish when we could, and cook what we caught over makeshift fires on the beach. Every meal was a mix of sea and spice: grilled sardines, steaming couscous, bowls of lentils, and the occasional tagine scored from a roadside café.

I remember Essaouira. Ancient ramparts rose above the sea, seagulls wheeling through pink dusk skies, the call to prayer echoing between stone alleyways. And then we rolled into Taghazout.

Back then, Taghazout wasn't the yoga retreat-littered surf town it is today. It was raw and quiet. Just a handful of rusting vans parked by the cliffs, their owners cooking canned beans and cleaning their boards in the chill morning air. The wave at Anchor Point was like a freight train. Fast, steep, and relentless. And it broke right in front of a nasty-looking jetty.

I paddled out on one of their borrowed boards, wearing a spring wetsuit that didn't quite seal right. The water was icy, biting through neoprene like a knife. I remember duck diving and feeling like my brain had been flash-frozen.

But when that wave came, peeling down the point like a silver ribbon, I dropped in, legs pumping, heart hammering. I rode it clean until it jacked up near the rocks. One misstep and I could have been shredded. But I bailed OUT just in time, the spray trailing behind me like confetti.

"C'était fou!" Julian screamed from the rocks at the jetty, throwing both fists in the air.

"Insane," I gasped, paddling back out, teeth chattering but soul alight.

The surf break called Anchor Point at Taghazout was a challenging wave, a fast and hollow right wave. I could only compare it to Todos Santos on steroids in the Baja South peninsula of Baja California.

We stayed in Taghazout for a few days, waking before dawn to glassy sets, sleeping crammed into the van at night in a pile of sleeping bags and damp towels. Then, hungry for new adventures and emptier breaks, we pushed farther south past Agadir, toward Tarfaya and the edge of the Sahara.

Now we were deep into what was once called the Spanish Sahara, now the disputed French Sahara, a ghostland of wind and sand. There were military checkpoints and the occasional whisper about tensions with Mauritania. But for us, it was all about finding waves untouched by tourism, wild and unspoiled. And we did.

We set up camp just off the coastal cliffs south of Tarfaya. The van doors opened to the Atlantic, and we would sleep under stars so dense it felt like you could scoop them with your hands. The morning sun would rise like fire over the dunes, painting the sand in hues of gold and blood.

One night, after a long surf session, we sat around a driftwood fire eating grilled mackerel wrapped in tin foil.

The flames crackled and danced, lighting our salt-crusted faces.

"Have you ever read Wind, Sand and Stars?" I asked, pulling the tattered book from my backpack.

Luc leaned forward. "The guy who crashed in the desert?"

"Yeah. Antoine de Saint-Exupéry. French pilot. Got lost out here. Almost died. But he described it all like poetry. The silence. The beauty. Even the loneliness."

Didier nodded, staring at the embers. "This place, it's the same. You feel like nothing and everything at the same time."

That's exactly how I felt, every night and every morning in that remote corner of Morocco. The wind howled, the ocean roared, and in between it all, we were just drifters sleeping beside eternity. Out there, under that sky, the idea of borders, of politics, of names, all faded. There was only the wave, the wind, and the warmth of shared purpose.

The war zone signs reminded us we weren't just off the grid. We were off the map. But that danger, the edge of the unknown, only sharpened the clarity of the moment. We didn't belong to any country out there. We belonged to the sea.

That safari changed me. Not just the waves, but the silence of the desert, the camaraderie with strangers, the rawness of sleeping under stars with sand in your teeth and

salt in your blood. That was Morocco, in 1984. And I carry
it with me still.

Chapter 5

The Rip Current Miracle

The Frenchies had decided to venture out of the towns after a tense encounter with some locals at the bustling market square. The incident happened after they, in their naive curiosity, decided to try smoking the famed Moroccan hash. It was an impulsive move, one I had warned them against, but they were charmed by the idea of an authentic experience.

We had driven into one of the larger towns, parking our dusty van near a noisy Zouk market teeming with life. The air was rich with the scent of spices, grilled meats, and sweat. Narrow passageways between vendors pulsed with color and energy. Brightly dyed fabrics fluttered in the wind, copper pots reflected shards of sunlight, and goats bleated near crates of citrus fruits. It was chaotic, alive, and somewhat overwhelming.

We wandered among the maze of stalls until we came upon a cluster of coffee and tea shops tucked along a side street, where the pace was slower and the air thick with the smell of mint and tobacco. It was there that we were approached by a couple of local hustlers. They were smooth, persuasive, and spoke with eager smiles that barely concealed their intent.

"Come, friends," one of them said, gesturing warmly toward his shop. "Try our tea. The best in town. And maybe a little treat to go with it, yes?"

The Frenchies, eager and a little reckless, nodded eagerly. I followed reluctantly, my gut telling me this might spiral into something I did not want to be part of. I was never a smoker and was seriously contemplating leaving the group altogether if they continued chasing these dangerous highs. But there was an undeniable truth ringing in my head. Safety in numbers.

I knew that on my own, I would be far more vulnerable, especially as a foreigner, even if I blended in with my long curly hair, sun-darkened skin, and casual stride. That did not stop someone from stealing my brand new hiking boots I had bought in Holland, right off the beach while I was surfing. I looked like a local, but I was still seen as prey.

At the coffee shop, three of us sat with the Moroccan hosts, sipping on hot mint tea served in delicate, flowered glasses. The heat of the day clashed with the warmth of the tea, but it was strangely comforting. One of the hosts pulled from his pocket a block of hash. Dense, dark, and clean, easily 100 grams of what the Frenchies called la bonne qualité.

I sipped my tea in silence while the negotiations began. Words flowed back and forth, animated hand gestures coloring the scene. In the end, a deal was struck. One hundred francs, a pair of tennis shoes, and a French T-shirt worn, but apparently valuable enough to seal the arrangement. The Moroccans nodded in agreement.

"We bring it to your van," one said, flashing a grin. "Thirty minutes. Then all is done."

Our other two French friends had stayed back at the van, so we made our way there. But when we arrived, the van was unattended. No sign of them. A strange stillness settled around us. Then, from the shadows, the Moroccan returned, but not alone.

He brought two towering men with him, both of them broad, silent, and dressed in dark clothes. They flanked him like sentinels. The main hustler's demeanor had changed. Gone was the light-hearted charm.

Nevertheless, we invited them inside the van in order to make the trade of goods.

He approached with feigned confidence, his eyes flicking around nervously, and a thin, deceitful smile stretched across his lips as he pulled the hash from his coat pocket.

It was a smaller piece, duller in color, and clearly not what we had seen earlier. He placed it in his hand like it was gold, but we were not blind.

One of the Frenchies leaned forward and narrowed his eyes. "That's not the same hash," he said bluntly. "That's maybe half the size. And the quality is different."

The Moroccan threw his hands up in mock indignation. "It is the same!" he snapped, his voice rising. "Exactly the same! You insult me."

I pulled a small keychain scale from my pocket, a mini balance I kept more as a curiosity than for practical use, but it now had a real purpose. "Let's be sure," I said calmly. I first demonstrated it with a 100-gram French coin to show it worked. Then, slowly and deliberately, I hooked the new piece of hash to the scale. The needle dipped. Only 50 grams.

The truth hung in the air like static. Silence followed, thick with tension. The Moroccan's eyes flared. His face twisted in fury as he smacked the scale from my hand. "This is not a real scale!" he yelled, spit flying.

At that moment, the two men at the entrance to the van started lifting their shirts just high enough to reveal the daggers clipped to their belts. They did not say a word. They did not have to.

My heart thumped hard in my chest. For a split second, I thought we were going to be robbed, or worse. Then, like a scene from a Western, our missing two Frenchies returned. Muscular and tan, they leaned over the entrance of the van and were in control of the situation. One of them cracked his knuckles and said coolly, "Is there a problem, boys?"

Now we were five against three. The power shifted. The Moroccans glanced at each other, calculating. The tension eased, but only slightly. The French calmly took the 50-gram piece and offered 50 francs and the T-shirt, nothing more.

The Moroccan stared at us hard but knew he had been caught. He snatched the money and shirt with a scowl, then turned sharply, muttering curses under his breath. They walked away, but lingered around the corner, speaking to some other locals in hushed tones.

"We need to leave. Now," I whispered. "They'll bring the police. Or worse."

It was common knowledge that the hustler dealers would sometimes sell you to the police in order to make a double profit.

The French did not argue. We jumped into the van, the engine groaned to life, and we peeled out of the town, leaving the market and the hustlers behind us.

After that harrowing experience, we made a vow. No more large towns. No more back alley deals. We turned south and found peace in the endless stretch of what was then the Spanish Sahara. The contrast between the golden sand dunes and the deep blue of the Atlantic Ocean was otherworldly. Out here, the world slowed down. The danger fell away.

On Christmas Eve, I found myself separated from the Frenchies who had dozed off, stoned and oblivious, inside the van. I wandered along the coast and stumbled upon a group of local fishermen camped near the shore. Their huts were made of driftwood and palm fronds, and a soft fire glowed at the center of their small circle.

They all seemed happy to see me as though I were one of their brothers. One of them smiled and motioned for me to join. I accepted. The air was cool but not cold, and the stars above shone with crystal clarity. The ocean murmured behind us.

We sat around the fire sharing fish soup, fresh baguette, and surprisingly decent red wine. They spoke in simple French, broken but warm. Laughter echoed over the flames. Then someone brought out the shisha, ornate, fragrant, and ceremonial. When my turn came, I took it in hand, lifted it to my lips, and pretended to inhale. I was asthmatic and knew I could not risk it, especially not tobacco mixed with hash. But they did not notice or did not care. We passed it around like a peace offering.

Then, just before midnight, they beckoned me toward the sea. The moon hung full and heavy above the water. We walked barefoot on the cold sand, down to the shoreline where their nets lay. I helped them haul in seven long, heavy fishing nets. There was only one catch, a small shark, still wriggling in protest, but they did not seem disappointed.

That night, surrounded by honest, kind-hearted men under a starlit sky, I experienced one of the most beautiful Christmases of my life. When it was time to leave, we clasped hands and exchanged grateful MERCI for their hospitality.

I walked back alone, the Frenchies still snoring in their van. I did not need a flashlight. The moon guided my way. The stars seemed to sing. I felt full, full of something that had nothing to do with food or wine. It was peace, clarity, and maybe even grace.

I whispered a thank you to the universe. To God. For that moment. For that night.

But I had no idea that by the next day, I would once again be calling out to the Creator for help. And this time, I would need it more than ever.

Chapter 6

Drowning in the Atlantic

In the early hours of the morning, I was abruptly awakened by the thunderous crashing of waves, like distant cannon fire rolling through the damp mist. The rhythmic roar was unrelenting, primal. I sat up inside the tent, stiff from the night's chill, and pushed aside the flap. What I saw stopped me mid-blink.

We had unknowingly pitched camp beside a majestic, untouched surfing spot, a crescent-shaped cove with jagged black rocks guarding part of the shore like ancient sentinels. The waves were perfect, heavy, double overhead sets rolling in with precision, the kind of clean, glistening walls of water that surfers dream about. But they were also frigid. The Atlantic here didn't lie. It was raw, wild, and 13 degrees Celsius cold.

I rummaged through my gear and sighed. All I had was the borrowed spring suit, a short 2mm wetsuit more appropriate for temperate spring breaks, not subarctic surf. Still, the temptation was too strong. The call of the sea overpowered caution.

I zipped up and turned to the French guys I had been traveling with, windsurfing fanatics more at home with sails and salt spray in the Mediterranean.

"Who's paddling out with me?" I asked, flashing a grin as I slapped the back of my neck to wake up my nerves.

They all shook their heads in unison, crossing their arms like they were guarding against a blizzard. One of them muttered something in French about froid de canard, duck cold.

"French pussies," I said, grinning. They burst out laughing, knowing I didn't mean it with malice. We were boys, bonded by travel and recklessness, and with that, I turned and ran headlong into the Atlantic.

The cold hit me like a wall of needles. The first duck dive was a punch to the soul. My ribs tightened. My breath shortened. My skin tingled like it was being peeled off. But I paddled hard, aiming for the clean outside sets before the chill overtook me. I had about 30 to 45 minutes before the cold stole my muscles.

On the second wave, I popped up, clumsily wobbled, and then I wiped out. My limbs felt stiff and alien, not responding fast enough. Hypothermia was already setting in. Then came the thunder.

A larger set slammed into me before I could fully rise, blasting me straight down. The ocean's power grabbed hold of me and tossed me like a rag doll. It felt like I was inside a washing machine from hell, flipping, tumbling, churning in a fury of whitewater.

I opened my eyes underwater, but it was chaos. No light, no direction. My lungs were starting to plead. I clawed to swim upward, but my sense of direction was scrambled. I kicked, only to find the sand. I had swum downward.

Panic surged in my chest like fire. But then a voice, calm and collected, rose up from somewhere deep in my memory.

"Serenidad y paciencia. La mente lo domina todo."

Peace and serenity. The mind controls it all.

Kalimán, the Incredible Man, my childhood hero from comic books, had returned to me in my hour of need. I closed my eyes and slowed my breath, telling myself to remain calm and wait. The ocean would eventually let me go.

Seconds dragged like minutes. But finally, the pummeling eased. I pushed upward. My lungs were about to burst when I finally breached the surface, coughing violently. Sweet oxygen. My salvation.

But something was wrong. The waves had died down. There was no surfboard in sight. I spun in circles. My yellow board was gone. My leash had snapped.

Panic returned with a vengeance.

I began swimming toward the beach, but my arms, my arms felt like overcooked spaghetti, flimsy, limp, useless. I couldn't lift them above the surface. They flailed more than they paddled. My legs, still functioning, kicked hard. But I wasn't moving toward land. In fact, I was drifting out.

The invisible hand of the rip current had grabbed me. I hadn't seen it earlier in my rush to ride as many waves as I could. I had ignored the cardinal rules of surfing.

Always read the ocean and identify the rip currents.

Never surf alone in a new, secluded spot.

I had broken both rules, drunk on adrenaline and ego.

Now I was paying the price. And I knew it.

Further and further out, the cliffs grew smaller behind me. The water deepened. The sky above mocked me with its innocence. My mind turned darker.

Is this how it ends?

Drowning, alone, unnamed in a disputed war territory, or would I be taken by one of the men in grey suits, great whites, common in this part of the Atlantic?

Floating on my back now, I could only kick gently, trying to angle parallel to the current to avoid being dragged deeper. But my kicks were getting slower. My body was heavier. My jaw trembled uncontrollably.

I tilted my head to the heavens.

"Diosito, ayúdame" I cried aloud. "God, if you do exist, please help me. I promise I'll be good. I'll call my parents. Just don't let me die like this".

Tears warmed the corners of my eyes for a second before freezing against my cheeks. I hadn't spoken to my parents in over two years. Rebellion had its reasons, but suddenly, none of them seemed worth it. Death has a way of revealing what matters.

I whispered more prayers between shivers. I was strangely calm. Maybe this was it. Maybe no one will ever know what happened to me. Maybe they'll just find my clothes in the tent or nothing at all. I accepted that I was going to die either by hypothermia and drowning, or be eaten by the great white sharks. Just as despair anchored me deeper, I saw something. A golden flash.

It glowed faintly on the horizon, bobbing toward me in the swell like a lifeline sent by God himself. My borrowed surfboard, the bright yellow surfboard, was returning to me.

I blinked. I wasn't hallucinating. It was real. The rip current that had been dragging me to my death had also delivered my salvation. Whether by divine grace or cosmic coincidence, I didn't care.

"Gracias Diosito, muchas gracias," I said while hugging and kissing the surfboard.

I latched onto it and hugged it like a long-lost friend, kissed it like it was holy. I must've looked like Tom Hanks with Wilson in Cast Away. Pulling myself onto the board with the last of my strength, I kicked and paddled, wobbling through the whitewash until the beach sand crunched beneath me.

I collapsed on my knees and kissed the cold, damp sand. "Gracias diosito, gracias," I said again, Elated for being alive.

Behind me, the ocean kept roaring, indifferent.

Back at the tent, the Frenchies were joking, laughing, blissfully unaware of how close I had come to being fish food. Luckily, they hadn't seen the board floating in. If they had, they probably would've grabbed it, thinking it was lost, and unknowingly sealed my fate.

Knowing them, they might have even burned my stuff and fled the area, fearing police or military trouble. I wouldn't have blamed them. We weren't supposed to be here. The signs at the end of the road were clear.

Disputed War Territory. Enter at Your Own Risk.

But we had entered anyway, and I had learned the ocean always collects its dues.

Chapter 7

Surfing to Hawaii and the Molokai Madness

Anyway, back to my 2004 Pacific Ocean crossing sailing adventure.

Our voyage had been surprisingly calm and uneventful for the most part. The sea had been generous, the winds kind, and our spirits high. Day after day, the endless blue horizon surrounded us in every direction like a never-ending dream, equal parts thrilling and hypnotic.

About halfway through the crossing, somewhere around 1,300 miles from either side of the Pacific, the ocean was as flat as a polished sapphire. The sun cast glimmers across the gentle swells, and the only sound was the occasional creak of the rigging and the soft slap of water against the hull.

On that tranquil day, something primal stirred inside me. I wanted to touch the heart of the ocean. So I tied myself up to a tether and safety line, took a deep breath, and dove into the deep blue abyss.

The sensation was electric. Floating in one of the deepest oceans on Earth with nothing beneath me but thousands of meters of mystery was both exhilarating and terrifying. My arms extended outward like wings as I bobbed in the middle of nowhere, suspended in nature's cradle.

The water felt heavy and endless. I could feel my heartbeat in my ears. I tried not to imagine what might be lurking in the depths below.

Then it happened.

"Shark. Shark," came the blood-curdling scream from the boat.

It was Boris and Harry yelling at the top of their lungs.

Panic surged through me like a lightning strike. I flailed with every ounce of strength, thrashing toward the ladder as if my life depended on it. I might as well have walked on water like Jesus himself. My heart hammered in my chest. My breath was shallow. My mind screamed one word over and over.

Survive.

As I reached the ladder and gripped it with trembling hands, I looked up, expecting to see chaos. Instead, I found those two bastards Boris and Harry doubled over, howling with laughter.

"Boris, Du bist eine Ashloch, I panted, still breathless. "You nearly gave me a heart attack."

Harry wiped tears from his eyes, grinning like a schoolboy. "You should've seen your face, mate."

I couldn't help but laugh through the adrenaline crash. That was sailing life. Fear, fury, and fun all rolled into one floating tin can.

On the 19th day, just as our spirits were beginning to wane, we sighted the peak of Mount Kilauea rising through a veil of thick clouds on the Big Island of Hawaii. Even cloaked in mist, the volcanic peak had a powerful presence, like a sleeping god watching over the Pacific. It was majestic and surreal, and it meant one thing.

We had made it.

We cracked open the iced bottle of good tequila reposado El Fogonero that we had been saving for this very moment. The cork popped like a victory salute. We passed the bottle around the cockpit, cheering and shouting to the wind. Salt-crusted faces broke into wide smiles, eyes rimmed with tears. That tequila never tasted so smooth.

But it wasn't over until the fat lady sang. We still had to cross the scary Molokai channel.

Ten hours later, we were sailing surfing 15 to 20-foot wave faces as we charged into the infamous Channel. The tequila buzz hadn't worn off, but we were riding high on something more potent now. Adrenaline and the nearness of land. The Molokai Channel is no joke. It is one of the most treacherous passages in Hawaiian waters. You cannot just cruise through it. You have to motor sail with a storm trisail rigged, manage your speed with surgical precision, and surf each wave like a pro to avoid pole pitching or capsizing the boat.

I had seen Harry handle it on our first crossing. His grip on the wheel, his feet braced, his eyes reading the sea. Being a surfer myself, I understood the rhythm of waves. I knew how to drop in on the face, angle the hull just right, and pull out before the choppy, steep waves closed out on us.

That final stretch was an adrenaline-fueled dance with death and the most exhilarating part of the entire voyage.

By the time we reached the Ala Wai canal, night had wrapped the island in a soft darkness. We navigated with the guidance of the Hilton's glow and the channel lights, eyes peeled for the dreaded Three Sisters. Or as Harry liked to call them, the Three Bitches. Three jagged, nasty rocks guard the right side of the entrance like angry trolls. Harry had hit them once on one of his three solo crossings. He never let himself forget that event.

Our bodies were wrecked. Muscles ached. Eyes burned. Yet somehow, we managed to drag ourselves off the boat and stagger our way toward the Harbor Pub in search of burgers and cold beers. We walked like drunken pirates in zigzagging S-patterns, legs unsure of solid ground after nearly three weeks of dancing with the sea. The tequila didn't help either.

We inhaled our food like starving castaways. I will never forget Harry, who, after being asked if we wanted dessert, propositioned the cute waitress to eat her out like an ice cream on the table, to which she just laughed and called him a dirty grandpa. Then we stumbled back to the boat, crawled into our bunks, and collapsed. I don't remember falling asleep. I just remember waking up 24 hours later to a pounding on the hull.

It was the men in blue uniforms, U.S. Customs.

We were so deeply asleep that it took them several knocks and shouts before we stirred. They weren't amused.

We were supposed to check in immediately upon arrival. We gave them our apologies and paperwork, groggy but compliant.

Fatigue at sea is a beast unlike any other. In the air, jet lag might chew at your senses after 16 hours of nonstop flight. But at sea, the exhaustion creeps in slowly and buries itself deep. We had been sailing for 19 days. There is no such thing as a full night's sleep out there. At least not for me. Thirty-minute power naps. Maybe an hour if I was lucky. Being responsible for the boat and my crew kept my mind awake even when my body begged to rest.

I remember one time I was trying to catch a nap in the aft cabin when I was jolted awake by a loud bang. My heart dropped. My first thought was a submerged shipping container. Every sailor's nightmare. I shot up and popped my head out of the hatch.

There was Harry, our Popeye, lounging in the cockpit, beer in one hand and cigarette in the other, like he was on vacation.

"Oh, don't worry," he said, completely unfazed. "Everything is under control. I think we hit a wine bottle floating by."

A wine bottle.

I glanced at the main sail and realized something was wrong. The sail was pointed in the opposite direction. I frowned.

"What's our heading?"

"West, of course," he replied, waving casually.

I made my way to the cockpit and looked at the compass. His face turned pale as he followed my gaze.

"Shit," he blurted, jumping to his feet. "We're heading north. How did that happen?"

The preventer we had rigged had apparently failed, letting the boom swing across with a wind shift. No one had noticed. Or maybe it happened the same moment we hit that supposed wine bottle. Either way, it wasn't catastrophic. At five knots an hour, we hadn't gone far. We corrected the sails, reset the heading to the southwest, and moved on.

Another time, while Boris had his three-hour watch, I was trying to sleep in my berth. I heard a bip-bip-bip-bip sound coming from the salon area.

I jumped up and looked at the radar screen. It was detecting traffic within the ten-mile ring that I had set up.

I yelled at Boris to look behind him because he was very casually sitting, looking forward. As he turned to look towards the back, he yelled, "Sheisse, how did that suddenly arrive?". I jumped out to the cockpit area and took the wheel, swinging it to the left. It was a container ship from the Watson shipping company, full of cars, that was headed at around 20 knots per hour (versus our 5 knots per hour) on a collision course straight towards us. I paralleled my heading when there was enough distance between us and the passing humongous ship.

These large ships aren't necessarily on the lookout for the occasional small sailboats. Sometimes they can't even detect us. And it has happened in the past when a small sailboat was rammed by a large container ship and didn't even know they hit it, or pretended not to have seen it, and they just continued on their way.

That would have been a disaster had we been run down by that ship. It would have cracked us like an eggshell and sunk us within seconds.

That was the rhythm of the sea. Long stretches of stillness punctuated by moments of raw chaos. Much like flying, the journey could be described as long moments of boredom interrupted by sheer flashes of terror. But boredom was rare. There was always something to do. Something to fix. Something to prepare for. Our boat was alive, and she kept us busy. We had guitars, bongos, books, and card games. We passed the time in laughter, in music, in deep conversations beneath the stars.

By the end of it, we were more than a crew. We were brothers. Each of us had earned a nickname. Boris became Boris the Horrible, also known as Galley Bitch for his flair in the galley. Harry, always calm with a smoke and a beer, was Popeye. And I was Capt. Bligh, the infamous a-hole captain from Mutiny on the Bounty.

We may have been worn out, salt-soaked, and sunburned, but we were alive. We were storytellers. We were sailors.

And we had crossed the Pacific.

Chapter 8

My Humble Beginnings

My life unfolded a decade at a time, shaped by the places I lived, the dreams I pursued, and the lessons I learned.

I was born in the early 1960s and spent my childhood growing up in Southern California. Back then, I was filled with dreams, big ones. At first, I wanted to be an astronaut, but after watching a commercial jet plane crash land at Ontario airport, I decided to be a pilot. I'd look up at the sky, watching planes cut through the clouds, imagining myself in the cockpit, chasing the stars. That sense of wonder stayed with me.

In the 1970s, as I entered my teenage years, I found myself living in Mexico. It was a time of discovery, of trying to stay out of trouble while navigating the uncertain edges of adolescence. Mexico was vibrant but full of distractions. I knew I had to get back to my original path. So in 1978, I returned to California with a renewed purpose, ready to pursue the childhood dreams I had carried with me for so long.

The 1980s brought a new set of challenges. It was the post-hippy era in California, and temptation was everywhere, fantasy, indulgence, sex and drugs, and rock and roll. I made a conscious choice to stay grounded, to keep my dreams alive, and to stay away from a life of debauchery and morbid temptations.

During the early eighties, I also took time to backpack across Europe, living freely and embracing the spontaneity of youth. Along the way, I met young frauleins and belle mademoiselles who made the journey even more unforgettable. Life was raw and real, and I loved every minute of it.

Through all the highs and lows, I remained focused, honest, and hardworking. I supported myself through an incredible range of jobs, fruit picker, carwash attendant, waiter, landscaper, Safeway clerk, pharmacy clerk, driver, gymnasium attendant, street musician, and construction sheather. I did whatever it took. Eventually, I completed my university degree in Airway Science and earned both my Commercial Pilot and Flight Instructor Certificates.

In the 1990s, my dream finally took full flight. I began my professional career as a pilot, first flying for a corporate operation and then for two Mexican airlines. I spent six years flying in Mexico, gaining experience, perspective, and a few unforgettable memories.

One of those memories came during my final corporate flight, departing from the Puerto Vallarta Aerotron FBO in a Sabreliner jet alongside Captain Tron. Just after takeoff, the jet caught fire. Miraculously, we managed to return immediately to the departure airport. Captain Tron executed an outstanding emergency landing, despite a complete hydraulic leak caused by the fire in the aft empennage section.

It wasn't until later that night that we realized how close we had come to dying. We were lucky not to be carrying fuel in the center tank. If we had been, we would have exploded in midair. And because we were still at a low altitude, we were able to minimize our time in a burning aircraft. When we inspected the damage, we discovered the elevator control cables had all popped, except for one single strand of wire holding the elevator together. That thread kept us in control, barely.

What still sends chills down my spine is the nightmare I had the night before. I dreamt I was killed in a plane crash. That eerie dream pushed me to review the emergency procedures for fire in flight, something that very likely helped us survive.

My time with the other two Mexican airlines was far less dramatic, but not without the extraordinary. While flying for Aviacsa, the first airline I worked for during that period, I encountered something I still struggle to explain. One morning, we were climbing out of Monterrey City on a route bound for Juarez, near the border of El Paso, Texas.

As we passed over a place known as the Area of Silence, we saw six bright lights hovering over the mountain ridges. That region has long been rumored to attract unexplained phenomena, and that day, I saw it firsthand.

Those bright lights soon transformed into white discs, clearly visible flying saucers flying right next to us in a floating formation. Six of them. I contacted Air Traffic Control, asking if there were military exercises in the area.

They responded that there was none, and then they asked me what I was looking at. When I responded that I had six round bright objects to my left, there was only silence. Then, in the blink of an eye, they vanished. Just like that, poof. One second, they were flying parallel to us, and the next, they were gone at the speed of light, streaking away faster than anything I've ever seen. Back to wherever they came from.

Chapter 9

Wings Across the World

It was in 1992 when we first saw them. Bright lights in the sky, strange and silent. That week, we saw them three separate times. The memory stayed with me, vivid and unexplained, a flicker of the unknown in the middle of my well-charted career.

Following my years with TAESA Airlines and Aviacsa Airlines in Mexico, I took a short contract in 1996 with Air New Zealand. I had decided to become a contract pilot. I made up an acronym that would meet my requirements and expectations of the contract and country I would choose. The acronym was "BBBW", meaning "beach, beer, babes, and waves".

And if it met all of the above, I was interested. That move took me even farther from home, across the Pacific to a land of clean air, rugged mountains, and the friendliest people I'd met. From there, my path led me to the exotic island of Mauritius. Flying there was like stepping into a dream, with sugarcane fields brushing the coastlines and the ocean below glittering like blue glass. But the best part was, it had many excellent uncharted surf spots. Especially Mandarin Bay, which was a popular, excellent surf spot.

After flying for Air Mauritius for nearly three years, I made my way back to the United States in the summer of 1999 to fly for a new startup airline in Las Vegas. I had had enough of Air Mauritius, and by the second year, I had a serious case of island fever. I couldn't see myself signing on for another three-year contract.

But thanks to my friend capt Brightman, who had recommended me for a direct entry captain position, I was able to make my move back to the States. It was my first command as a Boeing 757 Captain, and for three and a half years, I embraced the role with pride. But, like many ventures in aviation, the company eventually filed for bankruptcy, and once again, I was grounded.

In the early 2000s, after yet another airline folded, I found myself unexpectedly unemployed. But what came next would be the realization of a childhood dream. I landed a skipper position flying the mighty Boeing 747 out of Honolulu, Hawaii. It was the toughest flight training environment I had ever endured. We called it samurai fright training.

I even sailed my own boat across the Pacific to get there. I bought my first home in Kaimuki, nestled not far from Waikiki Beach and Diamond Head. By this time, I had a family of five, with my two youngest children born and raised in Hawaii. Life was full, bright, and brimming with meaning.

Since 1990, my flying career has carried me across the globe. I flew the Sabreliner jet for Aerotron FBO out of Puerto Vallarta, Mexico. I flew Fokker 100s and Boeing 737s, 757s, and 767s for Aviacsa and TAESA Airlines. With Air New Zealand, I operated the Boeing 767. At Air Mauritius, I stayed on the 767. Then came National Airlines out of Las Vegas, where I captained the 757. Later, I joined Japan Airlines as a skipper on the iconic Boeing 747 300 - 200 Classic.

Up until 2009, those were the major chapters of my aviation life. But from 2009 through 2025, I took on new challenges, flying for eight more airlines on short and long-term contracts. From the start of my airline career in 1990 until now, I have flown for a total of fifteen different airlines.

I have lived in twelve countries and earned Airline Transport Pilot Licenses from twelve aviation authorities, including the US FAA, and those of Mexico, New Zealand, Mauritius, Japan, China, Korea, Jordan, Ethiopia, Thailand, Maldives, and the United Arab Emirates.

Before all of that, between 1988 and 1990, I spent three formative years in general aviation, flying mostly as a flight instructor out of Montgomery Field in San Diego. Those early years built the foundation for everything that followed. I should mention that my first demo flight for a private pilot license was in 1981. I didn't continue because I had insufficient funds, so I put off flight training until 1986.

So what happened in 2009, when I was still living the dream in Hawaii, flying the Boeing 747-300 Classic for Japan Airlines?

The dream ended as suddenly as it began. In 2008, fuel prices skyrocketed around the world. The impact on Japan Airlines was devastating. By early 2009, while I was in transition training for the Boeing 747-400, all programs were frozen. We were told to go home and remain on paid leave as the company attempted to restructure.

The restructuring was swift and unforgiving. Japan Airlines retired all of its four-engine Boeing aircraft. One sunny morning, just after I had come in from a surf session and was enjoying coffee by the beach, I received an email. It simply stated that expatriate pilots were no longer needed.

The fallout was immense. Many of my fellow pilots had invested heavily in Razor FX, a currency trading scheme that turned out to be a scam. I had been suspicious from the start and decided not to invest. Most weren't so cautious. They lost huge sums of money. On top of that, several of them went through painful divorces. Some had fallen for our Thai or Japanese cabin crew members, left their families, and remarried these girls after a nasty divorce. It was a classic case of yellow fever, as we joked. It nearly happened to me, too.

Back then, I was still unmarried and in training in Tokyo. That's when I met Kaori. She was beautiful, with a radiant smile and a captivating Brazilian figure. A half-Japanese, half-Brazilian woman, fluent in English and full of warmth. She was much younger than me, but somehow it didn't matter. We spent several cold winter months together while I was completing training. In our free time, we traveled across Japan, riding the Shinkansen to charming towns and exploring hidden corners of the country.

Kaori made my time in Japan unforgettable. But when training ended and I was reassigned to Honolulu, the distance began to show. Slowly, we drifted apart, and eventually, we ended the relationship on good terms.

So much of my life has been shaped by movement, by flight, by change, by arrivals and departures. As I close this chapter, I stand at the edge of 2009, looking toward a new horizon. The next chapter of my life would begin not with a takeoff, but with another moment of reinvention.

Chapter10

The Ground Beneath Us

Now, the dream life I was living in Hawaii, six and a half years later, was coming to a sudden end due to losing our jobs.

The announcement came like a punch to the gut. No warning. No slow unraveling. Just cold, hard news that knocked the breath out of me. The moment the words left the manager's mouth, my whole world spun. It was as if everything I'd worked for had been snatched away in a blink. The shock of it sent a ripple through every part of my life.

That was a shock. The bad news ruined my whole day, and honestly, my whole month. My mind kept replaying it like a broken record.

Especially because now, I was married. To my longtime ex-girlfriend from San Diego. Life had come full circle in the most beautiful way. We'd had a wedding straight out of a postcard, a Hawaiian beach ceremony on the South Shore. White sand, a soft breeze, and the sound of crashing waves blended with laughter and vows. Her smile in the golden light of that sunset was something I can never forget.

But now, reality hit hard. I had five mouths to feed. A towering mortgage to cover. This wasn't just a setback. This was a storm.

Fortunately, the fact that our aviation broker, Wasinc, and the Japanese are very honorable and honest people saved us from complete despair. They gave us a generous end-of-contract bonus. And when I say generous, I mean it nearly covered an entire year's salary. It wasn't just money, it was a lifeline.

Still, I found myself in an unfamiliar space. Unemployed, or "in transition" as I tried to tell myself, for four long months. I didn't waste time. I tried everything.

One day, I was captaining delivery boats across turquoise waters, the salty wind in my hair, and the feel of the helm firm in my hands. Another day, I was hunched over my laptop, fingers pounding keys, chasing the rhythm of a book I had always meant to write. On others, I stood under studio lights, chasing another kind of dream altogether.

There was this show — "Lost." You know it. At the time, it was my show. Gripping, mysterious, unlike anything on TV. Imagine my surprise when I landed a small extra role. Even more surprising? They offered me a speaking role as one of the French people who arrived on the island. A real role. Lines, characters, story.

But Tokyo called. Recurrent training. I had to go. I passed.

Then, as if fate was testing me, they came back with a second offer. Another shot. Again, I said no. This time, it was the B747-400 transition course. My flying career seemed more stable, or so I thought.

Little did I know that just a couple of months later, I would be furloughed for good. If I had been psychic, if I had known what was coming, maybe I would have taken that part. Maybe I'd have leaned into the camera and said my lines like my life depended on it. Maybe, just maybe, I'd have carved out a second career as a part-time actor.

"Step aside, Antonio Banderas," I joked to myself one evening, a beer in hand as I rewatched my brief moment in season five. "Here I come."

Still, I did take on some background acting as an extra in Season 5, just because I loved that show so much. It was more than work, it was fun. A kind of therapy.

Meanwhile, life in Hawaii still had its magic. I had earned my Coast Guard 50-ton boat captain license and began to dream of a new chapter, trading in airplanes for ocean waves. I pictured myself chartering my own sailboat, guiding tourists past the glowing cliffs of Na Pali or into the hidden coves of the Big Island.

But dreams, as they say, don't always pay the bills. There was no real money in that.

So I turned back to what I knew best. I polished up my résumé, made it shine like a cockpit control panel, and started sending it out to airlines across the globe. I was looking for contract captain work wherever the wind and the job would take me.

Some of my old colleagues stayed in Japan, flying for smaller regional airlines. Others went back to the major U.S. carriers, starting all over again at the bottom of the seniority list.

I chose neither.

Instead, I stepped back into the world I had known best. Tax-free, international contract flying as a captain on heavy aircraft. Global skies.

I looked around the island one last time. The scent of plumeria. The hum of the ocean. My children are laughing in the backyard. The sun is setting behind Diamond Head.

"Goodbye, Hawaii," I whispered.

Then I turned toward the sky, toward the horizon, and toward whatever was next.

Chapter 11

Desert Skies and Shadow Games

Hello, flying in Jordan. 2009.

Flying contracts overseas isn't just a job. It's a lifestyle. A nomadic existence. It takes a certain kind of world gypsy to thrive in it, someone with thick skin and an open heart. It's not for the faint of heart. Not for homebodies tied closely to family, comfort, and the rhythms of routine life.

By then, I knew what I didn't want. I didn't want to start again at a major airline, a nameless cog at the very bottom of the seniority list, waiting years just to sit in the left seat again. I had already played that game, and I wasn't about to rewind the tape.

Back in 1993, I had interviewed with United Airlines. That experience? Brutal. It felt more like a Gestapo interrogation than a job interview. Cold stares. Rapid-fire questions. Judgment. I walked away thinking, never again.

Then came FedEx. Close, but no cigar. I almost made it in, but politics reared its ugly head. My sponsor, a captain friend, was at war with one of my interviewers. Union drama. Old grudges. That one decision, based on someone else's past, slammed the door shut on that opportunity.

Fast forward to April 2009. Out of nowhere, an old friend, Ron, from our days at the now-defunct National, reached out.

"How would you like to fly the 767 again?" he asked, voice warm with nostalgia.

"Where?" I asked cautiously.

"Jordan Aviation. Amman."

There was a pause. I let the name hang in the air. Amman. Jordan. The Middle East. I had always said I'd never fly in the Middle East. Not because of fear, but because it felt like a world apart from what I knew, a place so distant from home, culture, and the ocean.

But here I was, saying yes.

And so I flew out, hired alongside another familiar face, Allen, another veteran from National. We were in it together, diving headfirst into a new chapter.

The job was unlike anything I'd done before. Our primary mission: transporting United Nations peacekeeping soldiers across the globe. Congo, Sudan, Liberia. Flights to Saudi Arabia carrying pilgrims to Mecca. Holy flights, full of spiritual energy and quiet reverence.

But there was another side to these missions.

On one flight into the heart of Africa, I struck up a conversation with the commander of a UN unit on board. He was direct, not one for political sugar-coating.

"What exactly are you guys doing in the Congo?" I asked, more out of curiosity than anything else.

He looked me dead in the eyes.

"We're here to protect U.S. interests, the uranium mines. Peacekeeping is just the official line. We're making sure the Russians and Chinese don't move in."

The words hit me like a slap. So much for world peace. The blue helmets were just a cover for geopolitical chess.

I was in for more shocks.

Coming from a structured, honest, and respectful airline background, what I found in Jordan was, frankly, chaos. Disorganization, poor oversight, and a culture shock hit hard and fast.

A month in, my license and ratings were still tangled in bureaucratic limbo, waiting to be validated into a Jordanian ATPL. Meanwhile, I was alone, half a world away from my family. I missed my kids, my wife, the ocean, and the freedom.

There was one day I remember vividly. A grey sky hung over Amman. I walked into a Pizza Hut, hoping for something familiar, something that might bring me closer to home, even just for a few minutes. I ordered a Hawaiian pizza, ham, and pineapple, just like the kids loved. But the moment it arrived, I couldn't eat it. My throat tightened. Tears blurred my vision. I paid, stood up silently, and left.

I walked for hours that day. Through winding streets, past crowded markets and towering minarets, just trying to wear myself out so I could stop feeling so much.

Finally, after threatening to quit in my second month, they put me on the flight roster. Things began to shift.

The copilots were mostly younger, some from Middle Eastern countries, others from Europe. Eager, kind-hearted, respectful. I started to build new friendships. Ron and Steve became my anchors. Then there was Sonu, Khaled, and sweet Hady, a flight attendant with a gentle smile and a laugh that made the long hauls feel shorter. She was kind and sharp and reminded me of the lightness I'd been missing.

But not everyone was like that.

Mike the Frog, as we nicknamed him, was a problem from day one. Crude, cocky, and always on edge. One night, we were flying into Aleppo, Syria. A critical approach, high terrain, and nightfall. Mike was at the controls, but mentally, he wasn't there.

Earlier in the flight, I'd asked him calmly, "Hey Mike, make sure you speak slowly and clearly with ATC. They're not used to heavy accents." He got angry at me because I criticized his heavy Manchester ghetto slang that the ATC controllers could not understand.

He glared at me, jaw clenched. "You have control," he snapped, then stormed out of the cockpit and disappeared for two hours. Just like that.

I turned to Khaled, our second officer, and nodded. "Looks like you're up."

When Mike finally returned, he was groggy, still in a mood, but insisted on flying the approach. I monitored it carefully.

But then he did the unthinkable. He disengaged the lateral navigation and started twisting the heading selector manually, turning toward high terrain.

"I have control," I said firmly, hands already on the yoke. I corrected the flight path immediately, my heart pounding. That could have been the end of us.

But it wasn't just his flying. Mike had been harassing the Muslim flight attendants, making crude comments, and flirting inappropriately. It crossed the line.

One night in Aleppo, the hotel staff reported him. He'd been inviting reception girls to his room to party and drink vodka. That didn't fly in a conservative Muslim country.

He was grounded immediately and not long after, fired. Good riddance.

But before he left, he lashed out.

He spread a vindictive lie, telling management that Hady and I were secretly involved. A petty, baseless accusation. He just assumed something from the way we spoke or laughed together. Management questioned her, but in the end, nothing came of it.

Hady had four brothers who used to spy on her sometimes so which created a dangerous situation. Jordan

happened to have the highest number of honor killings in the
Middle East.

Still, it left a bitter aftertaste.

That was life now. Highs and lows. New friends, strange
cities, political games, and lonely nights.

But I was flying again.

And sometimes, that alone was enough.

Chapter 12

A Desert Christmas and Shards of Freedom

Still, it was a dangerous situation for her and me, more dangerous than most people would ever understand. She had those four controlling brothers. Not the teasing, overprotective kind you'd see in movies. No, these were serious, grim-eyed men, raised with the weight of tradition and tribal honor embedded in their bones, and in Jordan, honor wasn't just a word, it was a law etched deeper than any statute.

It is true that in 2009, Jordan happened to have the highest number of honor killings in the Middle East. It wasn't a statistic you read in passing, it was something you felt in the air. The threat was quiet but real. Everyone knew someone. Stabbing was the common way. Quick and brutal. No questions. Just silence and blood. And there was no repercussions from the law. It was part of the culture.

We were always careful. Eyes are always watching. Her glances were quick, her smiles hidden like contraband. A whisper here, a cautious look there. We lived like ghosts between concrete walls and narrow alleyways.

I was scheduled to fly to the Azores for Christmas with Hady and some of the Christian crew. The plan had been a perfect little escape, pine trees, salt air, midnight mass under old European stone.

But then, with no warning, they pulled me from that flight.

"Captain, you're grounded for now," the scheduler said with a tight smile. "South American captain's taking your rotation. Higher up's call."

"Why?" I demanded.

He shrugged, not even bothering to look at me. "Politics."

Politics. That's what they call ass-kissing now. And once again, the fourth law of Newton is in action. "Anything that crawls or kisses ass tends to rise".

So I was stuck in Amman for the holidays, bitter and boiling with frustration. Worst Christmas of my life. The rage had no outlet until it did. I grabbed the old rickety chair from the corner of the upper patio, its legs worn from years of sitting, and hurled it off my third-floor balcony. It spun through the air like a broken-winged bird and crashed into the empty lot below with a satisfying crunch.

I exhaled.

"Oh, that felt good," I muttered to the wind, hands still trembling. That's when the decision hit me with finality.

I was done.

I had had enough of the bullshit, the schedule politics, the loneliness. I hadn't seen my kids in almost four months. Time was slipping through my fingers like sand in Wadi Rum.

Then, something unexpected.

On Christmas Day, just after noon, my phone buzzed.

It was Chris, another American pilot stuck in Amman. He sounded chipper.

"Hey man," he said, "You wanna get outta here? Let's go to Jerusalem. Bethlehem. Let's at least make this Christmas count."

I hesitated. "You serious?"

"On the double, get ready. I already got a taxi waiting. Grab your passport."

An hour later, we were bouncing in the back of a yellow taxi, winding our way out of Amman, towards one of the northern border crossings that led to Bethlehem. The gateway to Israel.

Crossing wasn't easy. The Israeli border interrogation was meticulous. Stern faces, questions about every country I'd ever flown to, where I stayed, and who I met. Chris and I exchanged glances, wordlessly reminding each other to stay cool. After nearly two hours, we were through.

By the time we reached Bethlehem, it was 10 PM.

Cold desert air crept into our jackets as we stood before the great wooden gates of the Church of the Nativity. Closed. The birthplace of Jesus, two thousand years ago, is locked behind ancient stone and iron.

"Well," Chris said, lighting a cigarette, "that's that."

But across the street, a shisha bar flickered with warm light and laughter. Inside, the haze of apple tobacco floated over low chatter and glasses clinking.

We found a table by the window and ordered a bottle of red.

"To the baby Jesus," I said with a grin, raising my glass.

"To freedom, too," Chris added, clinking his against mine.

We smoked shisha, letting the warmth of wine and the hum of Arabic music fill the space where loneliness had been. Unexpectedly, it became a Christmas to remember.

Flying for Jordan Aviation had been wild and unpredictable. I made the best of it when I wasn't flying. I threw myself into the desert, getting lost in the ghostlike silence of Wadi Rum. I rode on horseback through the wind-worn canyons of Petra and floated like a beaver on its back in the still, salty waters of the Dead Sea. I watched the sun bleed into the Red Sea from the shores of Aqaba. The land felt ancient, wise, and secretive.

One unforgettable experience was on the night of my birthday, during a flight from New Delhi to Kathmandu.

We were ferrying an empty B767, and halfway into the flight, the flight attendants called me to come to the cabin. I passed the controls to the first officer and stepped out for a few minutes.

They had a cake for me and sang me the happy birthday song, in Arabic. How sweet that sounded. I had a quick tea and bite of the cake, said my thank you dearly, and returned to the cockpit to prepare for an intense high-risk approach into Kathmandu.

This approach from the south towards the north is one of the most critical high-elevation airport arrivals in the world. Why? Because the first few miles into the descent it is done at a very high descent rate in order to clear the high terrain and mountains in the approach path of the VOR RWY 02 approach landing to the north.

Then, fully configured for a landing, if the airport is in sight, we may continue for the landing. Or a missed approach if the airport is not in sight. Which is also a critical maneuver because it has to be done with a climbing immediate right turn to the south followed by a escape maneuver to the west, to avoid crashing into the Himalayan mountain chain to the north. (a Thai airways crashed this way some years ago, when the captain made a full 360 degrees turn instead of only a 180 degree turn to the south).

Anyway, there were a few cumulonimbus clouds generating some intense lightning, which in turn created Saint Elmo's fire on the windshield. It's a series of luminous electrical discharges of moderate intensity in the atmosphere. It's also plasma or ionized air that emits a glow of sparkling electrons in the air.

We had a spectacular display of st Elmo's fire during most of the descent. An array of beautiful psychedelic colors crashed against our windshield. That was my best birthday present from Mother Nature.

Reaching our minimum descent altitude, we had the airport in sight, and we landed. Later that night, from the balcony of my room facing the majestic Himalayas on this beautiful full moon, I opened up my mini bottle of good tequila and said cheers to myself and thank you, universe, for this beautiful experience.

Another great experience was crossing into Israel. Escaping to Jerusalem or Tel Aviv. It felt like stepping out of grayscale and into color. A five-hour bus ride over golden dunes, through lonely highway checkpoints, and then suddenly, bars, espresso cafés, bikini beaches, and people laughing openly in the sun.

I remember once walking along Tel Aviv's shoreline, the call to prayer still echoing in my mind from Amman, and thinking:

This is what breathing feels like.

Chapter 13

Surf, Borders, and Lines Not to Cross

Eventually, I found my people. Surfer friends who lived by tides and wind, not politics or dogma. Tel Aviv, with its salt-tinged air and late-night pulse, became a kind of refuge. It was a place where the noise in my head went quiet for a while. We were just watching the swell roll in, boards under the arm, waiting for that clean Mediterranean break.

I kept in contact with the crew, real locals, guys who knew when a swell was coming before the websites even caught on. Still, I checked MagicSeaweed and Surfline religiously. They became my weather prophets.

There was some solid surf to be had. From the old Dolphinarium ruins, where graffiti whispered of lost decades, to the Hilton Beach, always buzzing with energy, tourists, and Tel Aviv's version of laid-back chaos. And there were other secret spots too, the kind you only learned through respect and time.

I really liked it there.

I liked the people, their frankness, and their edge. I respected their survival attitude and how they lived like every day mattered. Life was never taken for granted in Israel. That gave the city electricity, a kinetic rhythm that I vibed with.

I also had a few good friends in the area, the kind you don't need to explain yourself to. Like Navi, my guitar friend. A spirit of her own kind. We'd take her guitar down to the beach, just as the sun melted into the sea. We'd strum a few chords, drink a decent bottle of red, and let the sea wind carry the music into the night.

Navi would sing softly in Spanish or English, and I'd sometimes join in, my voice rough from sand and surf. She was fluent in Spanish and loved Latin music. We were just two musicians under the open sky, backed by waves and stars.

But everything comes to an end eventually.

One of my last flights to Syria changed everything.

We were scheduled for a routine turnaround in Damascus. But when I approached the immigration counter and handed over my U.S. passport, the mood shifted instantly.

The officer took one glance at the cover and his face turned hard.

"No entry," he said flatly.

I blinked. "Excuse me?"

He leaned forward, tapping the edge of my passport. "No visa. Not allowed."

Never mind the fact that I was the captain of the flight, or that all my fellow crew had just cleared through. This wasn't about protocol. It was politics. An invisible war playing out at some Middle Eastern airports. The U.S.

president at the time, Bush, had made inflammatory accusations, painting Syria as a harbor for terrorists.

So now I was the face of that passport. That policy. That label.

I asked, "So what am I supposed to do now?"

The immigration officer pointed toward a metal bench bolted to the wall. "Sleep there until morning," he said without apology. "The supervisor comes tomorrow."

That's when I had an idea.

I pulled out my second passport, my Mexican one, and held it up. I said, Sir, actually, I have dual citizenship."

The man looked at me. His expression shifted slightly. He tapped his own skin, then pointed at mine. Then, surprisingly, he smiled.

"Welcome to Syria, brother," he said warmly. "But you still can't come in. The general crew declaration form already states you are entering as crew with A U.S. passport."

He raised his eyebrows. "However," he added with a grin, "we can arrange for you to sleep in the first-class lounge. Food and drink, non-alcoholic of course."

And they did.

I ended up sprawled on a surprisingly plush couch in the lounge, sipping hot mint tea and eating flatbread with labneh, wrapped in a blanket someone had thoughtfully provided. My copilot, Khaled, ever loyal, insisted on staying behind with me.

"I'll translate, I'll help," he said. "No one should be stuck alone in a Syrian airport overnight."

It was a small gesture. But in that sterile, uncertain space, it meant a lot.

By morning, his supervisor arrived. Tall, dignified, with a thoughtful gaze. He greeted me with a formal handshake and a quiet, "Welcome to Syria, Captain."

Before the war turned into headlines and rubble, Syria was something else entirely. On days off, I wandered the winding alleys and Zouks of Damascus and Aleppo, ancient cities that breathed history and poetry. I sipped coffee in 2,000-year-old courtyards, watched old men play backgammon under fig trees, and listened to a call to prayer echo against stone.

The assumptions we have in the West about the Middle East are mostly wrong.

The people I met were some of the kindest, most sincere humans I've known. Their hearts were wide open, their hospitality legendary. There was a deep soul to Syria, something unspoiled beneath the dust.

Eventually, I was recalled to Amman. New assignments, this time for South American flights.

But things took a dark turn again.

One of my flight attendants, Hady, had come down with a rough case of the flu. I found her one day slumped against the terminal wall, pale as ash.

"Are you okay?" I asked, steadying her as she tried to stand.

She nodded weakly. "Just dizzy... It's nothing."

But the next day, she fainted again, and I took her to a nearby clinic myself. Diagnosis: severe flu, dehydration, and exhaustion. Yet the company HR in Amman didn't want to release her from duty.

"She's fine," they told me over the phone. "Don't worry about the crew rest."

"But she fainted," I said, stunned. "She's not fine."

They insisted, coldly, bureaucratically, that I proceed as scheduled, that I overlook the rest violations. That I fly with a sick crew and look the other way.

I was at a crossroads.

My moral compass and my license were pointing in opposite directions. So, I delayed the flights. Just by a couple of hours, enough to make the rest legal. I did what I had to do to protect my crew and my conscience. The company wasn't thrilled, to say the least.

I drafted an email, carefully and firmly. I sent it to the Manager of Operations and to Captain Kangaroo, the big boss.

I told them plainly: I will not be part of an illegal operation. You're putting people at risk. I'm not flying with a sick crew that haven't had their minimum required rest.

There was silence for a day.

Then, finally, they backed off. Hady was allowed to return home to Amman to recover. It wasn't a victory exactly, but it was a line I refused to let them cross.

Chapter 14

Checkpoint Whispers

We weren't exactly flying in luxury. Being a low-cost airline, budgeting extended into every corner of our operations, including, apparently, cross-border crew logistics. Instead of a simple transfer flight, they arranged a taxi for us to drive across the breadth of Syria to Amman, Jordan. It was nearly midnight when our journey began, the desert roads cloaked in darkness, the headlights barely slicing through the heavy stillness of the Syrian night.

The ride was eerily quiet, just the hum of tired wheels rolling across cracked tarmac and our own uneasy thoughts. We were crossing a region that felt suspended in time and tension. The silence outside was broken only by the occasional silhouette of a watchtower or a lone camel in the distance, eerily lit by moonlight.

Eventually, we reached the border, a cluster of dimly lit prefab buildings and chain link fences separating Syria from Jordan. What should have been a simple crossing turned complicated fast. There, amid the cold flickering fluorescence of the customs checkpoint, we ran headfirst into another bureaucratic wall.

Apparently, I couldn't leave Syria.

The issue? I had entered as a crew member via Damascus Airport, and according to the border guards, that meant I could only leave the same way. Hady, sweet and determined, was with me. She had been allowed to return home to Amman to recover and had volunteered to act as my translator. But now, even she couldn't fix this with charm alone.

There were five customs officers in total, each more suspicious than the last. Hady, ever resourceful, began making her rounds, smiling, laughing softly, engaging each man with the kind of casual warmth that disarmed suspicion. I had quietly slipped a crisp hundred dollar bill into her hand before she approached the supervisor. She sat on the corner of his desk, chatting lightly, tossing her hair, letting the charm flow with practiced grace. She graciously transferred the $100 bill to him when they shook hands. After a few minutes of what I could only imagine were compliments and casual flirtations, he gave her the slightest nod.

We were through.

We crossed into Jordan as dawn began to lighten the sky behind us. The relief I felt was physical, as though my lungs could finally expand again.

Later, I would find out why this airport debacle had happened in the first place. A Syrian security officer confided in our chief purser during one of the Damascus to Jeddah flights. Apparently, the Syrian and Israeli security agencies, despite being official enemies, do talk to each other. Quietly. For security reasons. And they knew. They knew I had entered Israel on a separate passport. This had been my Israeli passport only because it had no Arabic country stamps on it.

The Syrian officer passed along a chilling warning. Tell him not to try entering Israel again. They were now aware that I had also been flying into Syria.

That closed the door, at least for the time being. I couldn't risk returning to Tel Aviv, not to fly, not even to say goodbye to old friends. It was a reminder that in our world, borders weren't just lines, they were secrets, traps, alliances wrapped in shadows.

The airline itself? High risk didn't begin to cover it. We operated two aging Boeing 767s and a couple of equally weathered 737s. Our destinations read like a war correspondent's résumé: the Congo, Kinshasa, Luanda, Lagos, Accra, Brazzaville, Abidjan, and Gabon's Libreville. Places where stepping out of the hotel without armed guards wasn't courage, it was stupidity.

I remember one layover in Yemen, back before the war. We had been sent to a remote beach hotel outside of Sana'a. The skies were golden that evening, the sea darkening with the dusk. Chris, the other pilot, and I were joined by three flight attendants: one half Egyptian who spoke Arabic, and two charming Ukrainians who stood out like strobe lights in that conservative landscape.

Our goal? Something simple. Beer.

The Egyptian Ukrainian flight attendant, tomboyish in style and demeanor, did the talking. After some hushed conversations with locals, she waved us over to a beat up double cab pickup truck. Two young guys, eerily resembling Osama bin Laden's college-aged cousins, grinned and invited us in. I hesitated. Chris, ever the optimist, waved me on, assuring me this wasn't his first desert beer run.

The further we drove out of town, the more nervous I became. I leaned toward Chris and half-joked, "If we get kidnapped, raped, and beheaded, just know it's your fault." We chuckled nervously. The two men up front kept chatting in Arabic, seemingly oblivious.

Eventually, we reached a hidden park. Beneath the trees, a small stand was set up, an unofficial liquor store, Yemeni style. They only had warm Heineken, but we weren't picky.

I offered the boys a six-pack in thanks. They declined with a grin. Even money for gas was refused. Their manners were impeccable.

Curious, I asked, "Do you speak English?"

They turned, smiling widely. "Of course, mate. We study at Oxford University."

I flushed, remembering the inappropriate jokes we'd made in the truck. They burst out laughing.

So did we.

They had just wanted to help, and probably, yes, to admire the flight attendants. They dropped us back at the hotel with a polite "See you next time." What could have been a nightmare turned into a warm memory, one I carry to this day as a reminder not to judge so quickly.

Not every destination was so benign. Some were ticking time bombs. Take Venezuela, for example. On one flight, we were tasked with transporting 290 UN peacekeepers from Maiquetía Simón Bolívar Airport near Caracas. The company, either due to ignorance or cost-cutting, used 75 kilos as the average passenger weight when calculating takeoff load. That might've made sense for Asian routes, but these were full-grown soldiers with heavy gear. Backpacks weren't even factored in.

That night, as we accelerated down the runway, I felt the aircraft struggle. We barely lifted off before the opposite end of the runway. One engine failure and we would've plunged straight into the Atlantic. Cold, dark, unforgiving.

I reported it. I sent a detailed warning email about the weight miscalculations. They ignored it. They didn't like being told how to run their operations. Not even when lives were at stake.

Back in Amman, the low season hit. Flights were drying up, and the company hinted they'd cut our pay unless we were actively flying. That was my cue. I handed in my resignation and applied to Ethiopian Airlines. They needed 767 captains, and my timing was perfect.

It took about a week to wrestle the three months' worth of unpaid per diems out of them. The morning of my departure, I finally received the check, sixteen thousand dollars in crisp U.S. notes. With no time to lose, I ran to the bank, cashed it, and stuffed the bills into my socks and underwear.

Then I was off to Hawaii for a breather, the tropics a surreal contrast to the chaos I'd just left behind. In the midst of that short break, I was summoned to interview with Ethiopian Airlines. The meeting was delayed by two weeks due to a tragic crash of their 737 out of Beirut.

But I got the job.

A new chapter was waiting.

Chapter 15

Lion Kings and Loose Bolts

Flying for Ethiopian Airlines in 2010 came with its own set of risks. The flying was intense, the routes relentless, and the fatigue was overwhelming. As many already know, the airline suffered fatal accidents in 2009 and, later, the infamous Boeing 737 Max crash. The signs were there long before.

Life in Addis Ababa wasn't easy at first. The streets were full of sick and hungry children, beggars on every corner, dust in the air, and a heavy layer of pollution hanging above the city. Still, the coffee was rich, the beer was cheap, and the people were incredibly friendly.

After I completed my training, I was called in from standby reserve for a night flight with four legs crisscrossing Africa. I had been on standby all day, and then, without much explanation, they mysteriously extended my duty period and assigned me to the flight. We ended up with a six-hour delay while still at the airport in Addis Ababa.

I was surprised when I met the crew. What was supposed to be an instructing flight for a new pilot had turned into a very different scenario when that pilot called in sick. Instead, I found myself paired with a senior Ethiopian captain who was less than thrilled that I had been rostered as the Pilot in Command.

From the moment we stepped into the cockpit, the atmosphere was thick with tension. The senior captain took the first officer's seat while the young Ethiopian co-pilot sat in the observer seat. The dynamics were awkward, and it was clear this captain wasn't happy playing second fiddle to a foreigner.

As we pushed back and started the engines, a warning appeared on the EICAS — Rudder Ratio. I knew instantly that was a no-go. I told the crew we couldn't proceed with that issue. But the senior captain started playing a game of passive resistance, acting like it was a training opportunity and questioning every step I suggested. I told him to follow the checklist, consult the Mel, and contact the company to confirm with the Master Mel.

We worked through the QRH checklist and procedures, though I already knew we weren't going anywhere. I accepted taxi instructions to avoid blocking the ramp and asked the co-pilot to call for a parking stand. I planned to loop around the taxiways and return to the gate.

Somehow, the senior captain misunderstood and thought we were proceeding with the takeoff. He erupted. His voice rose, his arms waved dramatically, and he postured as though he were asserting dominance, like some Lion King demanding his place at the top of the hierarchy. It's part of the culture, age, and rank carry great weight, but in that cockpit, it felt unsafe.

I assured him it was a simple misunderstanding due to language, but that only made him more furious. I calmly told him we were returning to the ramp. Once parked, I shut down the engines and asked the co-pilot to check our duty limitations. As expected, we were approaching the legal limit.

I turned to the senior captain and said we couldn't continue. He looked me in the eye and said, "We are going."

I stood up, grabbed my flight bag, and told him, "You are going. I wasn't hired to violate duty limitations or regulations." I offered a handshake, which he refused.

As I stepped off the aircraft, I noticed a few angry passengers were also disembarking behind me. They had clearly had enough of the situation.

The next morning, I met with the training manager, Khaled, and explained what had happened. I asked him what would happen in situations like this, and he was candid. The senior captain was one of their most experienced pilots. Even if he was wrong, they couldn't challenge him directly. I was about to become the scapegoat.

He even admitted the captain was fatigued, stressed from a recent divorce and bankruptcy, and had just returned home that same morning from a previous flight with barely any rest. But hierarchy was everything.

I knew where this was going. Ethiopian Airlines had a reputation for "harassment training," a tactic used to push unwanted pilots out. Sure enough, they sent me on a Boeing

757 check flight to Brussels with Captain Johanes assigned to line check me. He was famous for transforming in flight into Dr. Jekyll and Mr Hyde.

On the flight there, he began the usual routine of putting on pressure and nitpicking. But after the layover in Brussels, as we prepared to board the return flight, I pulled him aside. I told him not to waste his energy harassing me on the way back, because I'd be resigning the moment we landed. He backed off, relaxed, and ended up sleeping in first class for most of the flight.

The next morning, I walked into the office and requested to be released from my contract without penalty. I framed it as a need to return home urgently due to family matters, which gave them a graceful way out without involving disciplinary action. They accepted my resignation, and I was finally free.

Thank God.

I had never felt so fatigued and unsafe as I did flying for Ethiopian Airlines. I even predicted there would be another major accident waiting to happen. Sadly, I was right. Fatigue and various other factors, such as the misunderstood new aircraft system called MCAS, played a major role in the 737 Max tragedy.

Flying in Ethiopia was challenging, but it wasn't without its moments. The pay was poor, but the few months there allowed me to explore the country. I visited holy sites, the Entoto Hills, local bars like Memos, and witnessed a level of poverty that was heartbreaking. Children followed us through the streets, desperate for food or anything we could spare. We packed bags of goods to give away and tried to help where we could.

Despite everything, the people were beautiful. Their smiles were wide and genuine, even amidst the harshest conditions. It was humbling.

When the time came, I said goodbye to my friends Peter, Tom Spotts, and his crew, packed my things once more, and headed back home to Hawaii.

And no, I never had to wear that ugly green uniform again.

Chapter 16

Life and Lessons in China, 2010-2012

The warm, golden beaches of Hawaii had been a welcome respite. For a few weeks, life had felt perfect, my family, the sun, and the relaxed pace of island life. But as the days in paradise slipped away, reality crept back in. My new journey as a cargo airline captain in Shenzhen, China, awaited me.

Shun Fung Express had extended an offer I couldn't refuse: a role as a Boeing 757 cargo captain with twice the salary I had been earning at Ethiopian Airlines. My future was set in the skies, but the cost was leaving behind my family once more. My wife, ever close to her family, refused to join me in China, preferring to stay in the comfort of her family's embrace. So, there I was again, on my own. Once again, all by my lonesome. I couldn't help but hum the melancholic tune, a little wistful about the journey ahead. (It's a song by the Rainbow Warriors, Kino and Friends from San Diego, in case you're curious.)

Living in China, I quickly discovered, was a world apart from visiting. The sights, sounds, and smells hit me with a jarring force. As soon as I left the airport, I was greeted by the harshness of the streets: people casually spitting on the sidewalk and in the air, the guttural sound of clearing throats echoing in every corner, and the unmistakable, overpowering stench that clung to the air like a thick fog. Even the pretty bank tellers, always impeccably dressed, seemed to have that unmistakable doggy breath that made me wrinkle my nose in surprise. The taxis were just as bad, a fetid blend of sweat, stale smoke, unwashed bodies, and something else I couldn't quite place. I grimaced as I stepped in, thankful only for the air conditioning and the relatively smooth ride—except for the language barrier, of course.

But despite all that, there were moments of beauty in the chaos. The lights of Shenzhen at night gleamed like a sea of stars, flickering reflections off the ocean as I looked out from my three-bedroom condo in Shekou, south of the city. I had an incredible view of the Hong Kong territories, and when I wasn't flying, I tried to take it all in.

Flying for Shun Fung Express was a different story altogether. The company was friendly, especially to us foreign captains, but the real challenge lay in working with the Chinese copilots. Green. Barely 300 hours in the air, and suddenly they were thrown into the cockpit of a Boeing 757. They were smart kids, college graduates with all U.S.-based flight training, but their English skills left much to be desired. And their claims of flight hours? Questionable at best. During their in-flight training, they were allowed to crowd in up to three new copilots, and they would all take turns in the copilot seat. They then all logged in all the flight time as though they had flown all the time in the copilot seat.

The worst part was their arrogance. Every time I tried to give a correction, it was met with a contradiction or, worse, a dismissive attitude. They never carried suitcases on layovers, showing up to every meal in the same rumpled uniform, their eyes barely open from lack of sleep. And there was the constant arguing in Chinese over the intercom, completely disregarding our attempts to communicate in English. They even managed to sneak cigarettes into the aircraft bathroom, disregarding every rule in the book.

The frustration built day after day. I needed something, anything, to break through. And then I had an epiphany, The Dog Whisperer. I'd seen the show where Cesar Millan tamed unruly dogs with a snap of his fingers, a sharp "shhh" sound, and a gentle push. Could it work on humans, too?

So, I tried it. I raised my hand, snapped my fingers, and made the "shhh" sound. At first, they blinked at me, confused. But after a few attempts, I noticed something. They stopped arguing. They started listening. It wasn't perfect, but it was progress. At least they began respecting my experience as a foreign captain who knew the Boeing operations manual inside and out.

Months passed, six months in fact, before I could actually fly the Boeing 757 myself. In the meantime, I was stuck in limbo, waiting for my Chinese license conversion and resident visa approval. The bureaucratic maze was maddening. I had to prove I hadn't committed any crimes in the nine countries where I'd flown, which was nearly impossible. Half of the airlines I had worked for had gone bankrupt.

Things finally started moving after a subtle bribe by the company manager to the Chinese police commissioner. A fancy dinner and drinks were all it took to grease the wheels. The business of China, it seemed, was driven by gifts.

Despite the challenges, I found some enjoyment in the little moments, like surfing in Xi-Chong Beach. The guards would close the beach during typhoon season, but my fellow surfers and I were experts at sneaking past them. We'd hide behind the trees, slip by, and then sprint into the surf. I could feel the pulse of adrenaline as I paddled out, the wind howling, the waves rising higher and higher. Surfers from all over the world gathered there, a wild crew, always ready for the next big swell.

The beaches were filled with locals, too, but they had an amusing way of celebrating the sea arriving in their best Sunday clothes, only to strip down to cheap 50-cent underwear, with their girlfriends clapping and cheering them on from the shore, some even still in heels, stuck in the sand.

China had its quirks, but it had its beauty, too. The people were unpredictable. Sometimes rude, but other times surprisingly genuine, far more real than the hypocritical polite smiles of the Koreans I would meet in the near future. There was something refreshing about it, even if I didn't always understand their way of doing things.

Flying was a different matter. The constant delays, the flow control, and the restrictions on airspace, especially over military zones, were frustrating.

One night, I found myself held on the ground at Beijing Airport for what felt like hours. The tow vehicle was attached to the aircraft, but the driver had fallen asleep, and no amount of gentle prodding could wake him up. I tried flicking the navigation light, no response. So, I turned on the taxi light and pointed it right into his face. It worked. He jumped up like a startled rabbit and drove away, cursing me in Chinese for blinding him. 30 minutes later, his supervisor showed up and explained to me that his employee had to be taken to urgent care due to sudden blindness caused by the taxi lights. Bullshit, it was their commie unions that make them such woozies. I couldn't help but chuckle at the absurdity of it all.

Nevertheless, I had to write an apology letter to my chief pilot, stating that I wouldn't do such a thing in the future.

Another time, I overheard one of my copilots accidentally give the wrong altitude clearance, since they use meters, we have to convert them to feet. He was probably dyslexic, and he responded "clear to 4800 meters, instead of 8400 meters. If I had not caught the mistake, it could have put us in a dangerous mid-air collision with another aircraft. It was moments like that, where quick thinking saved lives, that made me realize the importance of clear communication.

The young Chinese copilots slowly warmed up to me. They may have been cocky at first, but over time, we formed genuine friendships. Most of them were good kids, just trying to navigate their new world, just like I was.

Eventually, after two years in China, I made the decision to move on. Korean Airlines offered me a direct-entry captain position on the Boeing 777. It was time to leave. The farewell was bittersweet. My Chinese bosses were not pleased, but in their own way, they wished me well, saying, "Welcome to China."

The departure was hectic, though. I had to pack up my life in Shenzhen. My bicycle had been stolen right from under my nose while I was enjoying a coffee, and I had to sell my surfboards, except for the custom-made red beauty that still lives with me in San Diego. My Vespa had almost been confiscated by the crooked cops, but I outsmarted them more than once, speeding away and dodging their attempts to steal it. In the end, I sold it for half what I paid, saying goodbye to that part of my life.

And just like that, I was heading back to sunny San Diego, back to the family, for now, at least.

Chapter 17

Flying in South Korea (2013)

Little did I know, all the horror stories I had heard about Korean Air were true because every single one of them happened to me. I passed the three-day interview, simulator test, and medical exams, and was given my "Welcome to Korean Air" letter of employment. But there was a catch. I had to pay for my own Boeing 777 rating.

Also, in the small print at the end of the contract, it stated, "If a passenger death results from negligence of the captain, he should be sentenced to the penalty of death or somewhere around a million dollars in fines and or life in jail." Gulp, that part I did not like. But I had to sign it nevertheless.

So, I took the plunge and spent $13,000 on a Boeing 777 rating at Boeing in Miami. The process itself was straightforward, but I had an unfortunate experience with my simulator partner, a general aviation private pilot who thought he could jump straight into a Boeing 777 just because he had the cash. After two simulator sessions, he hit the panic button and gave up, not able to handle the complexity of the aircraft. He bailed, but I still had to use up his already-paid extra hours.

Once I got my Boeing 777 rating, I moved to the Hyatt in Incheon and began training at the Korean Air Training Center. The ground school and simulator training were standard and easy because they were run by expat Western instructors, and that was a small comfort.

But things quickly turned sour once we moved on to the in-flight training portion. I'd heard from others who had gone through the same process that there were some telltale signs indicating who would be selected for "the slaughter." From the start, it was clear that they had already decided who they were going to fail, regardless of their qualifications. One of the signs was when they called you "handsome."

Another was being assigned an ex-military instructor who seemed to have an inexplicable hatred for expats. And, if your instructor's English was poor, as mine was, then you were in for a rough ride. They would misinterpret things you said, and even when you briefed something or notified them of a situation, they'd write you up for things they either misunderstood or simply made up.

The operational experience flights were a whole new nightmare. We had Korean ex-military instructors, tough and old-school. My first flight to Paris was a disaster. My instructor, who looked like an Asian version of Mr. Spock, started off as a neurotic jerk. I don't even remember his name—it could've been Captain We Too Low, Captain Holi Fak, or Captain Sam Ting Wong. Getting ready for takeoff from Paris, he was immediately upset because I accepted a runway change. He wrote me up, claiming we shouldn't accept such changes, even though I thought he had messed up the new taxi instructions.

Koreans, as I quickly learned, were terrified of change and insecure when it came to flying planes. And their limited English made misunderstandings worse. From the very first flight, this guy was giving me nothing but negative feedback. I remember him saying after the first flight, "I can already see you're not going to pass this training," to which I firmly responded that I was here to pass, and we still had many more legs to fly.

Things began to go downhill after a simple family conversation. He showed me a photo of a little girl, and I assumed it was his granddaughter. He did look a little old for his age. When I said, "Oh, how sweet, your granddaughter?" he frowned and snapped, "It's my daughter!" Oops. I tried to recover, but it was too late. I was now firmly on his "shit list."

The communication between us was incredibly frustrating. It felt like he was looking for any excuse to write me up. There was an instance where I was manually landing in increased rain and asked him to turn the wipers to intermediate. After asking twice, he finally complied. Yet, during the post-flight debrief, he scolded me for distracting him from his duties. I couldn't understand why, especially when I was flying the plane and needed assistance.

His response? "My duties are monitoring instruments," as if that were more important than assisting me in operating the plane systems when needed. I was manually flying in visual conditions, and he wanted to monitor instruments instead of helping. Total nonsense.

We had a liaison, a Western interpreter, who conveyed to us what the instructors thought. Apparently, my Mr. Spock thought I was arrogant and was making him work too much. The interpreter suggested I start asking for his opinion on every decision, to make him feel important. So, I tried that approach. I would politely ask things like, "Captain, how do you feel about requesting a higher flight level?" But his feedback to the interpreter was that I was asking too much and came off as weak.

At that point, he became even more of an asshole. He started raising his voice and even screaming at me. That's when I decided to be firm. I ordered him to do things in the cockpit politely but with authority.

The whole training process felt idiotic. During one flight to Singapore, we were cruising at FL320, and I suggested requesting FL340 because it would be smoother and more optimal. He refused, citing the flight plan's FL320 altitude. I insisted, pointing out that FL340 would offer a better ride, and we did climb to 34000, and I proved I was correct. Naturally, he lost face and wrote me up again. He claimed that I did not follow the company flight plan altitude.

In many Asian cultures, losing face is an immense blow, akin to losing honor or respect, and it can even lead to people taking extreme actions, like committing harakiri (suicide by self-stabbing). Now, I didn't think he would go that far, but it was clear I had upset him in a way that would cost me dearly.

I had a few friends from my previous airline, TAESA, who were already flying for Korean Air. They gave me some advice and tried to guide me, but it didn't stop me from feeling the full brunt of the Korean training system. My friends had it easier a decade before, and the new, harsher methods were clear when I was subjected to them. In the end, I felt like some of my Mexican amigos were more worried about how they would be seen if one of us failed the training.

Things finally came to a head when I was recommended for a check ride flight to Tokyo. The chief pilot, who just happened to be Mr. Spock's buddy from the military, came along as an observer. The flight started well, but as we prepared to descend into Tokyo, things took a turn.

Tokyo approach cleared us to descend to FL320, and I repeated the clearance to both pilots. I set the altitude on the mode control panel, pressed VNAV, and began the descent. But as we were nearing FL330, I saw traffic on the TCAS screen at FL320, the flight level we had been cleared to descend to, coming our way. I quickly told the training captain to verify the altitude, and at the same time, Tokyo approach realized their mistake and ordered us to maintain FL330. I already had my finger on the altitude hold switch, which I pushed once, but the descent continued due to inertia. And the chief pilot screaming to press it again would not make much difference.

So, I immediately disconnected the autopilot to level us off at FL330 manually, as the momentum was carrying us further down. But both pilots screamed in panic, "Noooooo. Do not disconnect!" I had no choice, I had to disconnect to make a more efficient and immediate recovery. When I reached FL 330, I very smoothly leveled off and re-engaged the autopilot.

When I explained that I had to disconnect to avoid a TCAS TARA event or a reduced vertical separation violation, the chief pilot responded, " I don't care about violations. At Korean Airlines, we do not disconnect at high altitudes. You know what happens when we disconnect at high altitudes." Apparently, they were so afraid of manual flying that they couldn't do it without causing a rough ride for the passengers. They literally hurt passengers due to their rough handling of the aircraft.

I calmly told him, "I know what happens when you disconnect (meaning when 'you' guys disconnect), but as the captain, I did what was necessary. I handled it smoothly and efficiently."

When we landed back in Incheon, the debrief took nearly an hour, and when the chief pilot left, he did so silently, like a fox stealing chickens. Shortly after, my instructor came to me, head down, looking at his notes. Before he even started the debriefing, I said, "Captain, please get to the point. I know what you're going to say."

Then, to my surprise, he said, "Captain Horta, I hate my job." He shook his head, looked at the ground, and added, "The chief pilot ordered me not to pass you. I'm sorry."

By this point, I'd had enough. I wasn't going to take the abuse anymore. I had already been in a shouting match with the previous mr asian Spock neurotic instructor, after he screamed like a madman and pushed my hand off the mode control panel, which in response, I screamed back at him, "Captain, do not touch me again, that is unprofessional". After that event, he became a smiling pencil assassin, reporting every little thing. No matter what I did now, I knew it was over.

Finally, when it came time for my checkride recommendation, he said, "I will not recommend you." I politely replied, "Thank you for your time."

Thankfully, I was assigned a new instructor, but now he had been ordered not to pass me.

It became clear that the Korean instructors had an agenda: to fail half of the trainees. This wasn't about skill; it was about their way of "getting back" at the airline, which had restructured its training department to Western standards. Pressured by the international civil aviation, due to their various air crashes, and killed hundreds of passengers in the process. Korean Air's infamous unsafe history in the 1990s still lingered, and they had no problem sabotaging the new generation of pilots.

In the end, even after the instructor told me that if I talked to the chief pilot, I would get another chance. But I no longer wanted to be there, so I resigned. I hated flying with those people. They were the most insecure pilots I had ever met, and by far the worst airline experience of my life. I was stressed, losing weight, and to this day, I can't even stand the smell of kimchi, their favorite food. It resembled rotten cabbage with chili, and it tasted like it, too.

Chapter 18

Maldives Flying 2013

In 2013, fortune smiled upon me once again, pulling me into another captivating chapter of my aviation journey. My global network of friends in aviation proved invaluable. An old friend, Steve from Jordan Aviation, had embarked on an exciting new venture managing Mega Maldives, a burgeoning airline nestled in the heart of the stunning Maldives. His invitation to fly for him as captain on the Boeing 767 was irresistible.

Arriving in Malé, I was immediately enchanted. Imagine an endless tapestry of sparkling turquoise waters dotted with lush green islands and atolls, shimmering beneath golden sunshine, paradise on earth. My joy was further amplified when I discovered many familiar faces among my colleagues, friends who had previously flown alongside me at Jordan Aviation.

Before moving, I eagerly researched surf breaks, a hobby I passionately indulged in. My search revealed Raalhugandu, the sole surf spot on Malé island, tucked into its southeastern corner. This local gem offered vibrant waves and warm-hearted, friendly Muslim surfers. Sadly, this magical break was eventually spoiled by the construction of the bridge linking the island to the airport, but in 2013, it was pristine, perfect.

Hunting for a place to live, I found an apartment that seemed tailor-made for me. Situated directly in front of a small round beach near a jetty, my bedroom window offered a spectacular, unobstructed 180-degree panorama of the ocean, showcasing the enticing surf break.

One leisurely afternoon, my curiosity piqued as I glanced out the window to see a group of dark shapes playfully bobbing in the shallows. Initially, mistaking them for sea lions, I decided to investigate. As I neared the shore, laughter erupted from me, realizing my amusing error: these were local teenage girls, entirely draped in dark burkas, joyfully frolicking in the water. I fondly dubbed them the "Ninja Beach Babes."

Having departed quickly from home, I could not bring a surfboard with me, but I quickly integrated myself among the locals, demonstrating genuine respect and interest. A friendly local surfer named Ahmed offered his assistance. "Come, my friend," Ahmed said warmly, guiding me through the winding streets to a dusty garage filled with forgotten relics of surfing past. Amid the battered collection, I spotted a promising 6-foot round-tail tri-fin, its nose and tail slightly damaged. "Only fifty dollars," Ahmed shrugged with a smile.

Eagerly, I patched the board with wax, my only resource at hand, and ventured back into the waves. The board handled beautifully on the steep swells. The thrill of riding Raalhugandu was unparalleled. Waves breaking to the right challenged surfers to clear dangerously shallow coral beds littered with sea urchins, while the left side offered slightly deeper, yet equally thrilling rides.

The Maldivian surfers welcomed me warmly, respecting my age and enthusiasm. There were also other popular surf breaks on the other islands, such as Pasta Point and Jailbreaks, but they were a boat ride away.

Later that year, I spent a week on my friend Andres the Spaniard's safari boat, surfing all those popular spots.

Life settled into a pleasant rhythm. Malé, picturesque yet compact, was lively with bustling motorcycles and colorful boats dotting its shoreline. The locals, resembling their Sri Lankan neighbors with long curly hair and warm smiles, were polite but reserved due to cultural norms.

My days revolved around surfing, kite surfing, diving, and snorkeling, marveling at breathtaking marine life, from gentle giant manta rays to amiable reef sharks and a kaleidoscope of vibrant tropical fish. Malé, with its strict rules prohibiting alcohol, pork, and dogs, felt restrictive to many, but those inclined to water sports thrived.

When craving relaxation and socialization, a short speedboat ride to Hulhulé Hotel near the airport offered a reprieve. This popular spot, teeming with expatriates, featured a lively pool bar filled with bikini expat girls and the city's best fried chicken. Occasionally, sneaking alcohol became an adventurous pastime, utilizing my crew privileges to cleverly disguise spirits in empty green tea bottles, greeting customs officers with a casual, "Chikoriya."

My flying schedule with Mega Maldives was an exciting routine, often taking us to bustling Chinese cities and vibrant South Korean metropolises. The long layovers in Chengdu introduced me to the beloved giant pandas, whose behaviors became delightfully familiar through repeated visits. I visited them so often that I almost knew every panda by name.

On our days off, we enjoyed lively gatherings aboard rented yachts anchored off Hulhumale. Imagine nights filled with music, dancing under sparkling disco lights, carefree dives into the luminous ocean from the yacht's third deck, and laughter shared among our cabin crew girls of various nationalities and fellow crew members beneath starlit skies. It was our floating paradise, a welcome break from the serene yet monotonous island life.

Exploring neighboring islands and hidden beaches via local donhi boats became another favored pastime. Each island offered charming accommodations, cafés, and picturesque vistas, providing perfect weekend escapes.

During one of these casual outings at the H and H Hotel, destiny introduced me to Vicky, a spirited, captivating, beautiful younger Russian chick who left an unforgettable impression. But that's a story for another day.

Eventually, Mega Maldives' operations diminished due to lost Chinese contracts, and despite my promise to Steve to remain at least a year, furloughs were inevitable. After initially declining Etihad Airways to honor my commitment, circumstances shifted. Etihad called again, coinciding with Mega Maldives' recall. Respectfully giving a proper two-month notice, I bid farewell to this enchanting chapter in paradise, grateful for the memories and friendships forged amidst turquoise waves and golden horizons.

Chapter 19

Flying In Thailand 2013

In the meantime, over in bustling Bangkok, a new airline was beginning to spread its wings. Asia Atlantic Airlines, AAA, not to be confused with Alcoholics Anonymous Airlines, was setting up shop with a small but ambitious fleet of Boeing 767s. The airline needed seasoned captains to help train its inaugural batch of flight crew. Mega Maldives, caught in a financial lull and grounding part of its operations, temporarily leased out some of its flight captains, and I was one of the four selected to serve as line instructors.

We were already in possession of uniforms, so they flew us to Thailand, Bangkok specifically, the chaotic, electric heart of Southeast Asia. I moved there with Vicky, the Russian chick I'd met earlier. I had technically adopted her after we met in a Male after she had quit her job at one of the resorts. So we flew together to Bangkok, and I started my new post as a B767 line flight instructor. On paper, it looked like a solid career move. In reality, it became a cocktail of paradise and peril.

Bangkok was a stark contrast to the peaceful Maldivian beaches. I found myself living near Sukhumvit Avenue, close to 8th Street, an area pulsing with life, neon lights, and the ever-smiling, kind-hearted Thai people. The air smelled of street food, grilled satay, hot coconut milk, and diesel fumes from the tuk-tuks that zipped past in every direction.

Night markets glowed with color. The city had rhythm, like a never-ending festival.

But after a while, the constant noise and overstimulation wore me down. I missed the ocean breeze and the surf, the hush of the islands, and the tranquility that used to greet me with each sunrise. Bangkok drained my energy more than it fed it. And Vicky, the woman I had once found so intoxicating, began to change, too. While we lived in Male', life was beautiful, and she had been a cool chick with no high demands, but all that changed in Bangkok.

At first, being with her felt like living a Bond movie, flying exotic routes, exploring remote islands, and sipping cocktails in beach lounges. Vicky had quit her resort job and moved in with me into my cozy apartment on the southeast corner of Malé, overlooking the jewel-toned Indian Ocean. The days blurred in a haze of sun, sex, and surreal beauty.

But paradise doesn't last forever.

With time, Vicky began to show another side. She started hanging around other Russian girls in Bangkok, glamorous, hardened types who seemed to live for status, money, and control. Soon, she adopted their mindset.

"I need this," she'd say, holding up a designer bag.

"I deserve that," she'd demand, pointing to expensive jewelry or clothes.

"Why don't you give me more spending money like my russian girlfriends get?" she'd pout, her tone more calculating than emotional.

The tension grew. I couldn't see it clearly then, but I was dancing on a tightrope. I was being pulled away from everything I valued, all for lust disguised as love.

One morning, as I dressed for a 6 a.m. departure, she stood in the doorway in her sexy negligee, her arms crossed, lips thin.

"You're leaving again?"

"I have a flight. You know that."

Her eyes flashed. "You didn't even touch me this morning."

"I didn't have time, baby, I will take care of you tonight."

Before I could finish, she hurled a ceramic coffee mug at my head. It shattered against the wall, splintering into a hundred jagged pieces. My heart thundered in my chest.

Then she gave me a naughty look and said with her strong russian accent, "You know how to make me happy".

Then came the story that changed everything.

It was after a few too many vodkas, her eyes glossy, voice low and raw.

"When I was a teenager," she whispered, "My gang and I stabbed a woman. She was abusing her children. So we wanted to teach her a lesson, but we beat her up more than planned, and eventually stabbed her to death.

Her mom had to send her to school in Japan to prevent her from going to jail. She later denied everything and claimed she had been drunk and didn't mean what she said."

I stared at her, stunned. She held out a small pocket knife, one she said she kept for protection.

"I'll castrate you in your sleep if you ever betray me," she said once, half-laughing.

Except it wasn't funny. Not at all.

I was unraveling. My hair began to fall out, alopecia, the doctors said. But I knew it was stress. The weight of a crumbling marriage, the chaos of my affair, the fear of what I'd become. And the fear of losing my children.

My wife and I had been separated since I left for the Maldives. And Vicky, with her dangerous charm, was nudging me toward divorce.

"I want to marry you, I want your babies," she'd whisper. "Forget her. I'll give you everything."

I almost did. I was, as the Aussies say, cunt struck, blinded by lust, wrapped in fantasy. But reality came crashing back one day when I broached the topic of divorce.

My wife didn't flinch. She had already seen photos of Vicky.

"Let me save you from your stupidity," she said, firm and cold. "That girl, she's young, she's pretty. But the moment she gets her green card and a few kids out of you, she'll dump you and take everything. There won't be a dime left for our children. No. I won't give you a divorce."

That hit me like a slap. It woke something up. I was throwing everything away, for what? Then came my decision to get rid of her, after I posed her the question of "What If", my two little kids want to live with me if we get married, will you be a good, loving stepmom?

Her answer was cruel, "Fuck no, your kids are your problem, I want nothing to do with them".

Up until now, my lower head had been doing all the thinking, but now my upper head took over. Then I opened my eyes and started formulating a way to get rid of her without getting castrated in my sleep.

Etihad Airways called for an interview. That became my escape hatch. A lifeline. I grabbed it.

When I broke the news to Vicky that I'd be moving to Abu Dhabi, I expected rage. But she was surprisingly calm.

Little did I know that she had secretly applied with Etihad as well, as a flight attendant. She was hired immediately. But I didn't know that until I arrived to start training that spring.

"I'll miss you," she said. "But maybe this is for the best."

I packed my bags, ready to start fresh, to be the man I had once been. I returned to San Diego, stood before my wife, and promised:

"If you move to Abu Dhabi with me, I'll be the husband you deserve. I'll put us back together. I swear it."

She agreed. And for a while, life started to mend.

But Wild Vicky wasn't done.

One December evening in Abu Dhabi, months after we had resettled as a family, she called me out of the blue.

"I just want to say goodbye," she said softly. "To thank you for everything."

We met at Costa Coffee. She looked radiant again, too radiant. She wore a tight red dress, heels, and eyes lined like Cleopatra.

"Come up to my place," she murmured. "Just one last cuddle. For old times' sake."

I shook my head. "No. I promised my wife I would be loyal. I mean it."

She pouted, but I stayed firm. We chatted for a while over cappuccinos. She looked disappointed as I stood to leave, but she hugged me tightly.

"You were the best boyfriend I have had, thank you," she whispered. Her voice trembled.

Nine months later, I got a video call from her on Skype. She looked glowing, euphoric.

"I have great news," she beamed. "I had a baby."

My stomach tightened.

"How old?" I asked.

"Three months," she said quickly. "Premature. Artificial insemination, back in January, after I left Etihad."

But something didn't add up. I did the math. January, and she had tried to seduce me in December. Had she tried to pin a baby on me? I asked her how old her baby was, and she showed me a photograph of a normal three month baby boy. Someone else had gotten her pregnant, and she was gonna try to pin it on me. Probably to blackmail me later with my wife, in exchange for child support.

So that's why she had tried to seduce me. I couldn't believe it. When I questioned her if she was pregnant when she saw me, her smile faded. She lashed out, angry, offended, defensive.

"I can't believe you would accuse me of that!"

Then, almost sweetly, she added, "But… would you be his godfather?" I stared at the screen, stunned. Godfather? She had tried every trick. Love, lust, guilt, even legacy.

I closed the call, heart pounding. The kid wasn't mine, and again, I was saved by the bell.

Chapter 20

Flying Through Isolation: Abu Dhabi 2014–2020

So now, back to the life of a contract pilot…

Living the life of a contract pilot has repercussions.

It's not just the exhaustion or the erratic time zones. It's the emotional disconnect, the gradual distancing from your family's nucleus. You leave home thinking you'll provide them a better life, but somewhere over the oceans, you begin to drift, not just in the sky, but from them.

If your wife is not emotionally present, if she isn't intelligent enough to understand the mental wear and tear, or loving enough to comfort you after a 14-hour haul, then the silence grows. A silence so vast it drowns the familiar rhythm of home.

And then loneliness creeps in.

That's when it happens. That human need, no, that fragile longing to connect again. Even little puppies need to be touched and petted sometimes. That's my excuse, and I'm sticking to it.

I moved to Abu Dhabi alone in 2014, just me and my suitcase full of clothes and dreams. The desert heat hit me like a wall as I stepped off the plane, but what struck me harder was the emptiness of solitude.

For the first four months, while training, I stayed at the Dusit Thani, a luxurious 5-star hotel with high-ceilinged marble lobbies, gold-embellished interiors, and the faint scent of oud lingering in the elevators.

But it wasn't the plush duvets or rooftop pool that caught my attention.

It was the people.

To my surprise, there were nearly 200 newly hired flight attendants staying at the hotel. Most of them were in their twenties, radiant, enthusiastic, and impeccably groomed, predominantly from Eastern Europe and parts of Asia. The hallways and lounges were suddenly vibrant with laughter, heels clicking on polished floors, and the occasional scent of jasmine and citrus perfume lingering in the air.

It was distracting.

Middle Eastern and Asian carriers still held onto that old-school belief in glamor and hospitality, unlike some Western carriers, where the glamour had long since evaporated.

Still, I knew better.

I told myself sternly, "Don't get into female trouble again."

So I focused on my training, staying late in simulators, revising checklists by the hotel pool, nursing espressos while others flirted in the lounge. But temptation was everywhere. It felt like some twisted divine test, like God and the Devil were both nudging elbows, smirking, betting on when I'd slip.

Once training was done, my family joined me.

We settled in a large, modern apartment near the Abu Dhabi Twin Towers, the city humming around us like a living machine of glass, steel, and desert winds. A year later, we moved to Rihan Heights, near the Zayed Sports Center. That place had charm, landscaped gardens, children's play areas, and families from around the world. The kids loved it. Even my wife smiled more often.

But the real gem was Al Muneera, where we moved for the last three years. Facing Yas Island, it was a fusion of modern Western design and coastal tranquility. Boardwalks weaved through beachfront cafes, and walkways embraced the sea. Expats strolled with strollers, joggers ran at dusk, and seagulls circled lazily above. We had access to a private beach, and my mornings began with cappuccinos beside calm waters while the horizon yawned in dusty orange.

Every year, we traveled together, twice a year, to different countries. Sometimes Asia, sometimes Europe. Those were the moments when life felt whole again. Etihad Airways offered more than a job, it gave us experiences. The expat community was strong, full of camaraderie. We built friendships that lasted, some that we still cherish.

But the country had rules. Strict ones.

You had to adjust quickly or risk being deported. For instance, drinking was only allowed with a license, which we never bothered to get. Somehow, that didn't stop us from buying alcohol at the liquor stores. As long as you weren't caught drinking in public or, God forbid, driving with even a trace of alcohol in your blood, you were fine, but the consequences were no joke.

Three months in prison followed by deportation for even one drop of alcohol while driving.

The UAE felt like a well-oiled machine, but it was monitored. You'd see antennas and radar towers dotting the skyline, especially in expat neighborhoods. Some were disguised cleverly as palm trees. I kid you not.

A source once told me:

"They monitor every incoming and outgoing social call. WhatsApp, emails… even your apps are filtered. It's all watched."

I learned the hard way.

One layover, jetlagged, tipsy, and bored, I got my company iPad and began browsing emails. I didn't think much of it. One of them was boasting about the new Etihad ad campaign starring Nicole Kidman for the Airbus 380 Apartment Class. This came right after they skipped our bonuses.

I grinned and typed:

"Now we know where our bonus payments went. No wonder."

Another email announced multi-million-dollar profits for the year. I typed:

"How about some peanuts for the peasants now?"

And a third one? About yet another VIP boss being hired. I laughed and wrote:

"Gentlemen, the problem persists. Too many chiefs, not enough Indians. And I mean the ones with a feather on their head."

I thought they wouldn't send. The screen even said: "Unable to reply." So I hit send anyway, a big mistake.

A week later, I was summoned to a meeting with the Deputy Chief Pilot. When I walked in, there was no smile. In his hand was a printout, a neat list of every sarcastic comment I'd made, along with the corresponding emails they were attached to. He glanced up and asked flatly, "Did you write these?"I swallowed. "Yes, but... I didn't think they were actually sent. The system said unable to reply."

He tapped the paper with his pen. "Security sees everything you touch, write, or read on these iPads. Even if it says 'not sent,' they see it."

There was a long silence.

I shrugged awkwardly. "I guess I was just... jetlagged. Trying to be funny. I didn't know I was being monitored that closely." "I apologize, and I can assure you it will not happen again."

He nodded slowly.

"We take this seriously. It could've gone worse, but we're keeping it internal. You'll get a verbal warning."

Then he slid a form across the table. "Actually… a written one. You'll have to sign this. No more sarcastic remarks. Understood?"

I picked up the pen.

"I understand. It won't happen again."

And that was the end of it.

Chapter 21

Waves and Wings of THE UAE

The beaches shimmered like strands of golden silk under the Arabian sun, vibrant and alive, bikini friendly, yes, as long as the women kept to the sand. The street, just beyond the boundary of the shoreline, remained more modest in its expectations. But Dubai always danced to its own rhythm.

I remember the carefree laughter echoing off the surf shop walls as we strolled a single city block to the beach with our surfboards at our arms, two cabin crew girls in tiny bikinis beside me, their flip flops slapping against sun-heated pavement. No one blinked. No one cared. That was Sunset Beach in Jumeirah in Dubai. That was our slice of freedom.

Those final three years were golden. Al Muneera was more than just a neighborhood, it was a life. Azure waters curled against the private beach, and our days unfolded beneath vast skies kissed by desert sun. Life felt flawless until the tidal wave of COVID-19 and what I called the plandemia crashed into it all, changing the world overnight.

Still, if I were to rank it, I'd say that time flying for Etihad, living that beachside life, was my second best gig, right after the dream assignment flying for Japan Airlines out of Honolulu. Those island years had their own magic, but Abu Dhabi held a unique kind of energy.

Etihad had become a nexus of old friendships. Many pilot buddies from earlier chapters of my flying career had converged here. We were a tribe in the skies, and I was privileged to command both the majestic Boeing 777 and the elegant 787 Dreamliner, two machines I loved for their power, range, and grace. We flew everywhere. My logbook read like a passport collector's dream. Each month, no more than five trips, but every one an odyssey.

A typical stretch would begin with a 16-hour haul to LAX or San Francisco, or a sun chasing journey to Australia. From there, it was Europe, maybe Frankfurt, Paris, or Rome, before swinging back across continents to Bangkok, Singapore, Hong Kong, or Jakarta. I'd top it off with a few regional runs, quick turnarounds to Bombay or Colombo, or maybe a surprise cargo flight to Africa or Europe.

Best of all? The lifestyle. Fourteen days off per month, on average. And every three days or so, I'd be back home for three to four days off, wrapped in the warm normalcy of family life.

Like I said earlier, and I'll say it again, Etihad's cabin crew were stunning. Every bit as glamorous as Emirates, but more attractive ones from Eastern European countries, and with a more down to earth vibe.

On layovers, we'd gather, a handful of us, for dinners and drinks in faraway cities, the kind of evenings that blurred time and borders. Whispers of the legendary crew parties floated around, stories of pilots who got lucky and got caught. Not my circus, but I'd heard the tales.

The wildcards were the Romanian and Moroccan girls. Gorgeous, yes. Dangerous? That too. Their reputations preceded them, beautiful, fiery, and with a gift for turning marriages into wreckage. They didn't just break hearts, they dismantled lives. I'd been warned, and I listened.

Vacation days were a passport stamp collection in motion. In those six and a half years, our family set foot in 13 countries — Italy, France, Spain, Portugal, Sri Lanka, Thailand, Turkey, Lebanon, Seychelles, Mauritius, Bali, Maldives, and Greece. Each destination layered new memories into our shared story.

Summers in Abu Dhabi were scorching, four months of relentless heat that sent Etihad families fleeing to cooler homelands. For us, it was San Diego and Mexico. But I stayed. Duty called. Still, I wasn't one to sulk. On my long stretches off, I turned solitude into adventure, embarking on surfari expeditions across the Indian Ocean.

One of my favorite escapes was the Maldives. There, my old surfer buddy Andres, the Spaniard who ran the 100-foot surf charter, welcomed me aboard like a brother. We'd bonded years ago when I brought him my Russian girlfriend's cousin, a token of goodwill that somehow cemented our friendship.

That week on his boat was unforgettable, six days of chasing perfect waves, partying under starlit skies, feasting on fresh caught fish, and trading stories with a wild pack of 12 surfers from Northern Spain and Australia.

I chased waves in Sri Lanka, Seychelles, Mauritius, and even Thailand. Though I hadn't surfed Bali since the early 2000s, the memories still echoed with each wave. One summer, I even took a surf trip to Lebanon and had been various times to Tel Aviv, yes, there's surf in the Mediterranean.

Surfing in Lebanon wasn't about the size or perfection of the waves, they were modest, 2 to 3 feet, perfect for longboarding. It was about the people. The warmth. The shared stock. I contacted a surf club before arriving, arranged a board rental, and booked a beachside spot. When I showed up, the "club" was a weathered brick hut, 20 boards leaning against sun worn walls, and not a soul in sight. I called the number from their website. A laid back voice told me to just grab a board and hit the water — "Pay me later."

Every morning or evening, I paddled out solo or joined a few locals. One was a 15-year-old Syrian refugee, wiry and graceful, carving lines like a pro. There were even three local girls surfing in full wetsuits despite the summer heat, committed and fearless.

When it came time to leave, I searched for someone to pay. No one. I called again. "Leave what you feel is fair," he said. So I slid a $20 bill into an old surf wax box in the drawer of a dusty cabinet and scribbled a thank you note. I followed up with an email to the club, letting them know.

There was only one dark cloud, the government's control of the beach. Local surfers weren't allowed to walk across the sand. Instead, they had to trudge down the shoreline to a jagged, rocky entry point to reach the waves. The rule was clear, violate it, and surfing privileges could be revoked entirely. It felt unfair, even cruel. Yet, the locals complied, smiles intact, spirits unbroken.

Chapter 22

Desert Waves, Skyward Dreams

In the heart of the UAE, a place known for its vast desert landscapes and towering skyscrapers, even the waves managed to find their way into the equation. It wasn't a surfing hotspot like some of the coastal powerhouses around the world, but there were still moments of bliss for those who craved the sea.

In Al Ain Wadi Park, there was a wave pool, modest yet satisfying enough for anyone seeking the feel of the ocean, if only for a fleeting moment. The waves here weren't massive, but they carried a kind of charm that made the park an unlikely, yet beloved, oasis.

And when the winds blew strongly from the northwest, there was a different kind of wave that appeared, one generated by the wind's energy. It was a rare gift, showing up about eight months out of the year, usually just once or twice a month, but when it did, it was enough to fill the hearts of the desert surfers with joy. These wind-driven swells were a reminder that nature could still offer surprises, even in the most unlikely of places. Those small yet decent swells brought surfers together, from all walks of life, creating a unique bond among them.

Among this community was our Etihad Surfer and Skater Club, a tight-knit group mainly made up of cabin crew and a few pilots. The camaraderie among the group was palpable, mostly made up of charming Etihad female cabin crew members, many of them beautiful and full of energy, the kind of people you couldn't help but want to spend time with. There was something about the contrast of the desert and the sea that made everything more meaningful. Surfing wasn't just about the waves; it was about the journey, the connection with nature, and the people around you.

Driving an hour across the desert from Abu Dhabi to Dubai, feeling the heat and dust swirl around as you made your way to the coast, was a ritual. The surf wasn't spectacular, but it didn't matter. It was about the experience, the camaraderie of spending time together, the early morning trips, and the shared moments after, sipping coffee and enjoying breakfast in Dubai, whether at Sunset Beach by the Burj Al Arab or Nikki Beach. These were the small escapes, the moments when life felt simple and carefree.

But even in a place as dynamic and full of contrasts as the UAE, not everything could stay the same forever. As with all good things, the fun came to an end with the arrival of the COVID-19 pandemic. The wave of uncertainty crashed into the world with a suddenness that no one could have predicted. In July 2020, the news hit 600 expat pilots, including myself, were let go due to the crippling impact COVID-19 had on the airline industry. Flights came to a halt, with only cargo flights remaining, and the airline no longer had a need for us.

The way Etihad Airways handled the situation left much to be desired. They took the decision to retire the most experienced captains first, starting with those of us in the near-60 age category, using reverse seniority. First, they let go of the troublemakers and those who had abused sick leave, but the financial hit was hard for everyone. Salaries were slashed by 50%, and the emotional toll was high. The pandemic wasn't just a global health crisis; it was a crisis of trust, and the rules felt like an imposition, stifling the spirit.

The isolation was perhaps the hardest part. After every cargo flight, we were quarantined for six weeks in Etihad accommodations, separated from our families. Every arrival from a flight brought the dreaded double nostril swab, a sensation that almost felt like it was trying to poke into the very depths of your brain. After each test, I would breathe a sigh of relief when the results came back negative, but the routine remained the same, stay away from family, stay isolated. The sense of confinement was suffocating, but there was always the escape, the fleeting freedom I could find if I was clever enough.

On more than one occasion, I managed to slip away from the watchful eyes of the Etihad security personnel, disguised with a hat and mask, leaving my phone behind so I wouldn't be tracked. Pedaling my bike out of the underground parking lot, I would head toward the place that mattered most: my family. These small rebellions felt like a reminder that, no matter how much the world around us tried to control us, there were still moments we could control.

The frustration and chaos of COVID brought with it a realization that, for some, it was all part of a greater plan, one that wasn't just about a virus, but about fear, control, and manipulation. The vaccine, a solution that was meant to end the crisis, seemed to many like part of a bigger agenda. In my eyes, it was a tool in a broader scheme to infect the population by creating new viruses and to line the pockets of those who stood to gain from the mysterious and suspicious vaccines that they suddenly created. The fear, the division, the uncertainty, it all felt manufactured, as though the people were being controlled, led like sheep to the slaughter.

But in the midst of all this, there was a strange sense of peace in the knowledge that I could walk away from it all. The layoff wasn't a devastating blow. In many ways, it was a door opening. With the end of my career at Etihad, we happened to be vacationing at our home in Mexico, near my favorite surf spot, Pascuales. The thought of an extended vacation, a time of relaxation and reflection, felt right. Early retirement, living off the rent from our properties, seemed like the next chapter.

But life, as it always does, had other plans. My old friend Mario, the Venezuelan, came through with an unexpected offer. He sent my resume directly to the Chief Pilot of a cargo airline in the U.S., and just like that, I was hired as a direct-entry captain on the Boeing 747-400. It was a fresh start, an unexpected twist in a story that had already taken some wild turns.

Through it all, from the waves in the desert to the uncertainty of COVID, the ups and downs, there was one constant: the journey. It wasn't always easy, but it was mine.

Chapter 23

The Divide Between Cargo and Passengers

Flying back in the USA felt like stepping into a whole new world after years of navigating through the skies of the Middle East and Asia. This time, the cabin was different, quiet, sterile, and filled with an emotionless hum. Unlike the chaos and drama of passenger flights, cargo was much more straightforward. There was no room for the social intricacies of keeping passengers entertained or dealing with unruly passengers. Yet, there was a certain sense of dullness, too. The air felt heavier in the absence of human presence.

I had flown cargo before, primarily in China, but never quite like this. Cargo flights were reliable in their predictability, but they lacked the human element that made flying with passengers feel more like an art form. Sure, cargo had its practical merits, efficiency, organization, and an almost monotonous routine. But it was the passengers who brought life into the skies. The contrast between these two types of flying was undeniable, each with its own set of pros and cons.

Flying passengers was a well-oiled machine, with each flight scheduled well in advance. You knew when you were flying, where you were flying to, and the days off you'd be granted. It was organized to a fault, almost military in its precision, which made the whole process feel seamless, though perhaps too rigid. But in that structure, there was a sense of order and reliability that was hard to argue with.

The social aspect of flying passengers was the sweet spot. You didn't have to dine alone in strange cities; you could easily make plans with the cabin crew for dinners and drinks. The conversations and camaraderie made the long hours and odd schedules worth it. After a flight, you'd find yourself sitting around a table at some restaurant, laughing and sharing stories of the skies, feeling that fleeting connection with people who shared your experiences.

But not everything was perfect. Passenger flights came with their own set of complications. The demands were constant: lost or irritable passengers, those who needed medical attention mid-flight, bomb threats, and the unpredictable moods of certain crew members. There were many times when the social perks of the job were overshadowed by the stresses of managing emotional passengers or dealing with an angry crew.

A memory from 1993 surfaced in my mind. I still remember that one flight attendant, who, after a fiery dispute over a personal matter, decided to spill coffee on my precious goods. However, I intercepted it with my hands. She had caught me in bed with one of the newbie flight attendants, and she wasn't pleased. I admit, I was young and reckless then, more focused on the fleeting pleasures than the consequences. In the heat of the moment, I had acted impulsively, and it led to a conflict that, well, didn't end in the most dignified of ways.

Another incident, this one from 2001, made my heart heavy every time I thought of it. A senior cabin crew member had taken it upon herself to administer oxygen to a sick passenger without notifying me. The lack of communication resulted in a dangerous delay.

By the time she finally came to the cockpit, the passenger was far worse. We had to descend rapidly after declaring a medical emergency with Air Traffic Control, and when we landed, a medical team was there waiting. They whisked her away, but I still remember her beautiful, green eyes and the gentle smile she gave me as if silently thanking me for getting her to the ground alive. Tragically, she passed away on the way to the hospital. If only we had known sooner, if only I had been notified in time, maybe, just maybe, I could have saved her.

Flying passengers often felt like walking a tightrope. Each day was a mix of careful planning and unpredictable chaos. The relationships between the flight crew and ground personnel sometimes added another layer of tension. In the U.S., there were often unspoken grudges, little dramas that erupted whenever we crossed paths with certain gate agents.

One incident stood out to me vividly. It was at the Las Vegas airport, while flying for National Airlines. The ground agent at the check-in counter tried to bump my son off the standby list. My 11-year-old son was number one in the standby list on my flight, but this particular agent, for reasons that were completely personal, tried to manipulate the list to get his boyfriend's parents onto the flight, even if it meant putting my son at risk of being left behind.

When I realized what was happening, I acted swiftly, demanding the agent remove the couple from the flight and ensuring my son was on board. His anger was palpable. He threatened to report me, but once MY report was filed and it became clear that his actions were illegal, he was removed from his position. It was a small victory in an often challenging world, but it reminded me of the power dynamics that could rear their ugly heads in the airport world.

Ultimately, it wasn't the passengers that I missed; it was the ease of the schedule and the sense of predictability. With cargo, there was no need to deal with the whims of impatient travelers or security personnel. But it wasn't without its own frustrations, either.

Cargo flights were efficient but lacked the spark of humanity that made flying with passengers feel alive. The TSA, especially, could make even the simplest part of the journey feel like an ordeal. The way some agents behaved, as though they thrived on their little moments of power over the passengers, was exhausting. It was almost as if the rules they imposed had more to do with asserting dominance than safety.

Cargo was clean, efficient, and detached. Flying passengers, on the other hand, was a world full of people, personalities, and problems. It was unpredictable but human. The one constant, though, was that I had lived through both worlds. And somehow, each had left an imprint, a lesson, and a story to tell.

Chapter 24

Cojones, Cargo, and Chaos

It was a few years back on an Etihad flight, somewhere in the middle of a short European rotation, when I found myself transiting through Amsterdam's KLM security area. The sharp chill of the terminal air mixed with the low hum of activity that never quite sleeps. My crew walked ahead, chatting, laughing lightly, probably thinking about layovers or coffee. I trailed behind, calm, composed, until I noticed a subtle shift.

Security officers scanned the crowd, then locked their eyes on me. Just me. Not my crew. Just the tall, dark, and handsome dude in uniform. (yeah right).

"Excuse me, sir. Step this way, please," one of them said flatly, gesturing toward a separate screening area.

I nodded, suppressing the familiar mix of annoyance and suspicion bubbling beneath my professional exterior. Was it the uniform? My kool and relaxed posture? Or just the color of my skin?

Maybe the captain might be a terrorist. Let's harass him more. Right?

After the standard X-ray machine ritual and the magic wand dance over my limbs, came the real humiliation. A security agent approached, stale breath reeking of cigarettes and cheap coffee with a thick Eastern European accent and a disposition somewhere between overly zealous and hostile.

He didn't speak much. He didn't need to.

Without warning, his hands started probing around my collar. Not a check. Not a pat. Groping. Rough. Invasive. Not at all procedural.

"Is that really necessary?" I asked, voice calm but edged.

He ignored me. His hands moved lower, aggressive, unchecked, until he dropped into a crouch. And then, with a flat palm, he slapped my private parts, my cojones, no less, with deliberate force.

A surge of pain. Disbelief. Anger. My body reacted before I did.

My left arm snapped up on instinct. A swift karate chop, right to the side of his head. Smack. He stumbled back and landed on his ass. No one gasped. No one came rushing in. But every eye within earshot now burned into us.

It was clear he meant to provoke me. And I wasn't going to let it slide.

Before he could call for backup, I stood tall, loud, and firm. "I want your supervisor. Now."

A few tense minutes later, the supervisor showed up polite, controlled, perhaps aware of the liability. He made the agent apologize, visibly uncomfortable as he did so, and assured me that "further training" would be required.

Further training. A euphemism for: "We know this was wrong, but we can't say it."

Flying cargo, on the other hand, doesn't come with these humiliating side-shows.

Less security theater. Fewer overzealous pat-downs. We're usually escorted directly to the aircraft in private airport shuttles. After the cargo's loaded, they fuel us up, drop off the catering, and we're wheels-up at least, in theory.

Reality? We're never on time.

Delays of up to six hours are common. Recently, we waited 10 hours on the aircraft due to an unplanned maintenance issue, before they let us go back to the hotel. But since our duty days can legally stretch to a monstrous 30 hours (thanks to a four-man crew and corporate greed), they push us to the edge every time.

Schedules change on the fly, literally 10 TO 20 times a day, and so do our destinations. We often end up flying into airports we've never even heard of, much less trained for. And when the crew isn't friendly, it's table for one. A long-haul dinner in silence.

However, most of our flights are crewed by a great bunch of guys and gals. Add to that rotating roster of new hires, inexperienced, underqualified pilots placed in the cockpit thanks to well-meaning but flawed equal opportunity hiring rules. The law says they belong there. But flying a 747 isn't about checking boxes, it's about lives.

We once flew with a confused earthling, a male-to-female transition person who was in that new-hire category.

Not only did we need to babysit her through procedures, we had to walk on verbal eggshells.

Once, during descent into a Polish airport, the first officer and I were casually talking about the charm and natural beauty of Eastern European girls, nothing crude, just light cockpit banter to keep spirits up. Suddenly, she leaned over the radio panel and smirked.

"What about me?" she teased, fingers moving toward her blouse. "Maybe I should show more cleavage."

I blinked. Did that really just happen?

Trying to maintain professionalism, I muttered, "I'm gonna pretend I didn't hear that," and focused back on our approach.

If it had been the other way around, if we had made such a comment? We'd have been crucified. But laws and HR policies have become blind to context. It's very clear who the law is going to take sides with, them, because airline companies are afraid of legal issues with these equal rights legal battles.

"To err is human," some philosopher once said. And in our line of work, errors come easily, fatigue, stress, the clock ticking past 20 hours. You name it.

One such blunder became infamous among us as "The Stairmaster Event", a comedy of errors at a Jordanian military airport that would've been hilarious if it hadn't cost over a million dollars.

The setup: Two "A" personality male captains with little or no social skills, two expat copilots, one foreign, dimly lit military base. Ground crew coordination? Nonexistent. Lighting? Pathetic. Morale? Lower than the runway lights.

In a rush to leave, no one noticed the stair truck was still in front of the aircraft. The ramp crew had vanished into the night, leaving the stairs, a full mobile stair unit parked in front of the engines. The tower couldn't see it. Neither could the crew.

They started engines, got taxi clearance, and rolled forward.

CRASH.

The aircraft clipped the stairs, knocking the entire truck over onto its side. And yet, they kept rolling, oblivious. Not until warning lights lit up the cockpit, indicating hydraulic failures, did they start suspecting damage.

When they taxied back, they spotted the stair truck lying on its side like a fallen mammoth. "How did that happen?" one of them asked, half stunned, half pretending not to know.

The aftermath? A million-plus in damages. Red-faced reports. And a new story was added to the cautionary tales of crew rooms worldwide.

That airport was jinxed. I swear.

Different night, same cursed tarmac. This time, it was me.

I was prepping for engine start in pitch-black darkness when I caught a flash of movement, the crew truck ahead of us suddenly dashed away like it had seen a ghost. That's when I felt it. A subtle shift. We were... moving?

Parking brake: confirmed. Engines: not started. So why did the cockpit feel like it was gliding?

I checked again. Was it an optical illusion? One of the other pilots was standing behind me, eyes scanning the ramp, when it hit us.

We were actually rolling.

The chocks had been removed without telling us, and the accumulator pressure had dropped too low to hold the parking brake. The massive 747 was now inching down the ramp toward the runway. Silent. Slow. Deadly.

The other pilot lunged forward, reached over, and switched on the auxiliary demand pump for System 4. We screeched to a stop, just short of entering the active runway.

That airport, those nights, those kinds of near-misses they leave a mark. Cargo may be free of nosy security checkpoints, but it's filled with chaos, unpredictability, and sometimes pure danger.

And yet, somehow, we keep flying.

Because up there, even when everything else is out of control, you're in control of the sky.

Chapter 25

Around the World in THREE DAYS

Flying a Boeing 747 into airports where jumbo jets don't usually dare to land. That's not just a job, that's an adventure.

This operation took us to the far corners of the Earth, touching down on everything from bustling international runways to isolated military airstrips surrounded by dust, wind, and sometimes armed guards. It wasn't your average point A to point B airline gig. It was wild, unpredictable, and every bit as exhilarating as it was exhausting.

There were weeks when we were literally chasing the curvature of the Earth, stringing together so many hours in the sky that time itself seemed to blur. We'd depart from Dubai, hop across Asia, skim over Pacific waters, dip into the Americas, and boomerang back across Europe or Africa, completing a full circumnavigation of the globe in less than four days.

Think about that. What Ferdinand Magellan set out to do over five centuries ago with his fleet of ships, we could accomplish in a matter of days. Of course, Magellan never finished it himself. He was killed and dismembered by the fierce warriors of Mactan island near Cebu island. It was Kano, one of his officers, who ultimately brought the expedition home, limping across the finish line after three grueling years with only 18 survivors out of the original 260 men.

And us? We might not be dodging spears or mutinying crewmen, but we're still fighting an invisible enemy every single flight: fatigue.

Jet lag and exhaustion don't just weigh down your body. They mess with your mind, your judgment, and your reflexes. And even though we're subjected to endless fatigue training videos and click-through computer modules, they're more of a box ticking exercise than real protection. Because the truth is, we're still being scheduled for duty periods pushing the 30-hour legal limit.

Why? Because if it's legal, the airlines think it's safe.

But it's not safe.

It's not okay to sit inside a metal tube for up to 30 hours, flying across different time zones, being constantly alert, managing takeoffs, landings, complex weather conditions, technical issues, and unfamiliar airports, only to be rewarded with a bare minimum rest period of 10 to 16 hours before doing it all again, and all of this, without proper hazard pay.

It's not just tiring. It's abusive.

I am now paying the price of 35 years of international flying, jet lag, irregular sleep, and irregular meals. But mostly, sleep deprivation has started to show in the form of arrested tremors in the right hand. (It's common in pilots who fly mostly international long-haul flights.)

This accumulated and chronic fatigue (CFS)opens up the arena so that when something finally goes wrong, a runway overrun, a bad landing, a misjudged approach, the first ones to be blamed are always the pilots. The captain specifically.

Not the schedulers, not the system, But The captain.

It's never just one error. It's a domino effect, a perfect storm of circumstances that begins with a fatigued crew. Maybe it's a new foreign captain paired with a rookie first officer. Maybe the aircraft is landing on a slippery, short runway with no margin for error. Or the brakes don't bite hard enough because of hydroplaning. It's always a series of things that build up like a snowball rolling downhill until it's too late to stop.

And yet, the Federal Aviation Administration, which claims to uphold safety, somehow allows this madness to continue. The irony is cruel.

It's not just us pilots. The engineers and loadmasters suffer even more.

Some engineers don't leave the aircraft for up to 14 days straight. Recently, I flew with a mechanic who had been on the aircraft for 18 days without setting foot in a hotel. Living like stowaways, sleeping wherever they can squeeze a snooze, on the upper cabin seats or on the floor on rolling mattresses, catching meals in flight, using wipes to clean themselves, and constantly at work. The aircraft and the crew depend on these guys to have a safe aircraft to fly.

Loadmasters are treated a little better, running like ghosts in the background to keep operations moving. Theirs is a very important job that assures the aircraft is properly loaded within the correct center of gravity.

The whole setup? It's modern day slavery in a polished uniform.

But speak up, and you're out. Quiet dissent is replaced by silence. Safety takes a back seat to schedules and profits.

A few years ago, British Airways conducted a chilling study on long haul pilots. The findings were nothing short of terrifying. The average lifespan of long-haul captains like me? Sixty-seven. Just two years after the standard retirement age of 65.

And the causes?

- One. Cirrhosis of the liver.

- Two. Heart attacks.

- Three. And tragically, a bullet to the head.

Yes. You read that right.

After retiring after decades of skyborne stress, only to face the dull reality of home life with a frustrated spouse and a body worn from years of jet fuel, airplane food, stress, and bad sleep.

"Honey, take out the trash," imagine hearing that for the remaining few years of your retired life.

You blink, half dazed, wondering how this domestic command replaces the tower's crisp voice clearing you for final approach. The contrast is too sharp for some.

Of course, the study did focus on British pilots, who, let's be honest, aren't exactly the poster children of clean living. They drink like it's a sport, smoke like chimneys, and eat enough bacon to feed a pub.

But it doesn't have to be that way.

We can change our fate, or at least try. I've taken my health seriously because frankly, no one else is going to. When you're living 35,000 feet above sea level half the month, you've got to build your own survival plan.

For me, that means yoga every day. Even basic TAI CHI stretches help ease the hours of sitting still. When I can, I follow it up with power yoga and mix in calisthenics to maintain muscle tone and flexibility. I walk as much as I can, especially in unfamiliar cities. Stair walking is a staple. When I'm home, I bike, surf, or skate, sometimes all three in a single weekend if energy permits. And if I've got something left in the tank, I'll hit the gym for a 30-minute free weights session. Because this lifestyle, this job, is already shaving years off my life. I won't let it take everything.

Chapter 26

Jet Engines, Cargo Dreams, and the Last Lap Home

Back in the rhythm of our flight operations, we operated like a well-oiled sky machine. Our crew composition was straightforward: four pilots, two engineers, and a loadmaster. Most rotations included two captains and two first officers, but often, the company would send us out with just one captain and three first officers. Those were the heavy runs, the fatiguing kind. You could feel the difference in your bones by day four.

We were on a 17 days on, 13 days off contract, home based. Seventeen days of flying all kinds of missions around the planet, then thirteen precious days to decompress, recover, and try to act normal at home.

And oh, the things we flew.

Everything from flowers to live animals, lithium batteries, textiles, medical aid, and once, even a rocket satellite, to Brazil. Then there were the mystery items. Huge, pointy, bullet shaped metal things, wrapped and sealed, destined for ambiguous corners of the world. Humanitarian aid, they said. But judging by the destinations, it looked a lot more like military logistics. We never asked. We just flew.

The cargo could be hazardous, dangerous, or unpredictable, but the job was never boring. We were the truck drivers of the sky, cruising the jet streams aboard the mighty 747, the Queen of the Skies. Every flight, every mission, was a new page in the adventure. That aircraft, with its elegant hump and thunderous thrust, was a pilot's dream. And it was mine, especially now, with retirement looming on the horizon.

I was less than a year away from retirement, and determined to close my nearly four-decade career at the controls of the 747. It felt poetic, really. I had flown nearly every Boeing except the 707, and now here I was, winding it all down on the most majestic one of all.

Thirty five years of airline flying. Twenty three thousand hours in the air.

By rough estimate, I had covered 11.5 million nautical miles. When you divide that by the Earth's circumference, roughly 24,900 miles, it comes out to about 460 laps around the planet. But factoring in all the changes in direction, weather diversions, and routing quirks, I figure I did at least 100 full east west circumnavigations of the globe.

That realization hit me recently during an 18 day rotation, a perfect example of the life we lead.

It all started in San Diego, where I caught a passenger flight up to Anchorage. After a night's rest at the hotel, I met up with the crew, four pilots, two engineers, and a loadmaster, and we boarded our Boeing 747 400 freighter. Our first leg: operating to Toronto.

After landing and clearing the post-flight overnight of a minimum of 10 hours. Then we boarded a commercial flight to Amsterdam in premium economy, switched to a connecting flight to Madrid, and endured a three hour ground taxi to our final destination, Zaragoza, Spain.

Zaragoza. A charming, sun-kissed city just east of Madrid. Narrow cobblestone streets led to bustling tapas bars, aromatic cafés, and open air markets alive with chatter and color. If only we had more time to explore.

Fortunately, this time we stayed three days in Zaragoza, and then we were back in the air. A straightforward cargo leg to Dubai Al Maktoum Airport, followed immediately by a 15 minute hop to Sharjah, then straight back to Zaragoza. If I remember correctly, we were hauling textiles that day.

Three legs, 26 total duty hours, and we never stepped off the aircraft. We rotated flight decks, shared the workload, and each pilot took a turn with a takeoff and landing. Exhausting, but that's how the job worked.

Our group of pilots was wonderfully international. A blend of backgrounds and cultures. Lots of Aussies from down under. Mostly men, but three real, strong women among us, (one of them my friend KC who is now a B737 captain with American). oh yeah, and a half male, half female earthling who is no longer there, all holding their own with professionalism and grit. There was something unspoken among us, a shared rhythm that built camaraderie. When you live, fly, and trust each other at 40,000 feet, you get close fast.

Of course, nothing ever stayed stable. Our roster changed constantly, sometimes several times in a single day.

One moment we'd be prepping for an eastern leg, and then boom, orders would shift and we'd find ourselves flying west instead. You learned to roll with it.

This time, we were lucky. We scored a 62 hour layover in Zaragoza. A gift.

Eventually, we pushed east again, this time to Hong Kong, where we checked into the Novotel Hotel for a proper 24-hour rest. Clean sheets, hot showers, and maybe even a glass of wine if we were lucky.

We usually stayed in five-star hotels, unless they were completely booked due to local events or tourist seasons. Which reminded me of a not so glamorous exception.

Last year, we flew a leg into Brazzaville, Africa, only to discover every five star hotel was sold out. A global economic conference had taken over the city. We were exhausted, and instead of luxury, we were sent to the only available boutique hotel, tucked deep in a rough neighborhood that looked more like the set of a post-apocalyptic movie than a tourist destination.

Rusting cars, some with no wheels, others with no engines, lay abandoned on the streets. Piles of debris and loose wires hung over broken fences. The air was thick with dust and diesel fumes. It looked like a place where time had stopped after a long fight.

But hey, no cockroaches.

The hotel was simple but clean. No bathroom door. No toilet seat. But the beds were firm, the AC worked, and we only needed to sleep for 10 hours.

So we locked our rooms, kept our shoes close to the bed, and hoped not to get kidnapped. We made it through the night, a little older, a little more experienced, and with a story for the next layover dinner.

This was the life. Never boring, rarely predictable, and always a little on the edge.

But I was almost there. Just one more lap around the world, maybe two. And then, finally, I could land for good.

Chapter 27

Across War Zones and Wave Dreams

We were back in Hong Kong. The buzz of the city seemed to hum beneath our feet as we made our way to the airport, minds steeled for what was shaping up to be another marathon duty day, twenty hours long. That's no small feat, even for a seasoned crew.

Our journey began with a heavy load, literally. The cargo was too dense to make the direct hop to Anchorage, so we charted our course Eastbound with a pit stop in Incheon, South Korea. It was just a technical halt, refueling, no time to soak in the culture or catch our breath. The engines barely cooled before we were airborne again, heading over the frigid Pacific to Anchorage.

In Alaska, the wind bit at our cheeks as we refueled once more, the ground glistening under the relentless twilight. The cargo ramp buzzed with efficiency while we stood momentarily still, wrapped in a bubble of silence and jetlag. Then, back into the cockpit and on to Los Angeles, where the Hilton Airport Hotel waited like a sterile refuge for the weary.

We barely closed our eyes for a minimum of 10 hours' rest before being routed again, this time deadheading to New York's JFK. The contrast between LA's sprawl and New York's vertical chaos was jarring. And no sooner had we landed, we were briefed. We'd be operating a flight to Tel

Aviv. Eyes widened. Even the most stoic among us exchanged glances.

"Didn't Iran just fire off missiles into Israel like...last week?" one of the crew muttered over coffee, his voice a mix of disbelief and concern.

"Yes," I replied quietly. "And again on October first."

The memories of that breaking news flashed across my mind, hundreds of missiles. But miraculously, only one casualty. Israel's defense, bolstered by the US, Jordan, France, and Britain, had intercepted most of them. Still, the tremor of uncertainty lingered. Thanks to the intercepting toys they acquired from someone, I wonder who.

The cause? A retaliatory strike. Two high-ranking generals from Hezbollah and Hamas had been taken out while hiding in Gaza and Lebanon. Iran, ever the puppet master of regional terror, responded with fury. To me, Israel's move felt justified. They're trying to decapitate the serpent, but it keeps growing heads.

The thought of Iran's unchecked nuclear ambition sends a chill through my chest. Fanaticism fused with fissionable material is a nightmare scenario, and one misstep could spiral into irreversible catastrophe.

Despite the unease, the company assured us there was no risk. "No hazard pay, but no danger either," they said.

We rolled our eyes. "Yeah, right," someone whispered. But we flew anyway.

Our cargo to Tel Aviv was officially marked as batteries and humanitarian aid, though we never see what's truly under those shrink-wrapped, netted pallets. It's always just a manifest and trust.

Once on the ground, the unloading was swift and tightly controlled. Military personnel in full gear took over while we stayed well clear, sipping burnt espresso in the safety of the crew lounge, stealing glances at the armored vehicles outside.

Two hours later, we lifted off again, this time for Larnaka, Cyprus, a quick 40-minute hop, but a world away in feel. The moment we arrived at the beach resort spa, it was as if we'd slipped through a hidden door into serenity.

The Mediterranean whispered against golden sands, and we, flight-hardened and adrenaline-worn, finally let ourselves breathe. That afternoon, we scattered in different directions like birds let loose from a cage.

But peace, as always, is temporary.

The next morning, we were told we'd all be flying to Amman, Jordan, as a team and then on to New York. A rare luxury, continuity. Familiar faces in the cockpit, shared jokes, camaraderie. But Scheduling had other plans.

A cold email alert lit up my phone. New assignment. I rubbed my eyes. "You've got to be kidding me…"

Each pilot was reassigned. Scattered like puzzle pieces across the globe. My new orders? Deadhead to Stuttgart and then Frankfurt.

I shook my head, muttering, "From Larnaka to Germany. That's a short leap." But life was full of surprises.

Still, I packed, boarded, and arrived. Exhaustion was creeping in.

Initially, I was told I'd be flying from Stuttgart to Houston and then to Anchorage. But no. Another change.

Now, I was a passenger again, deadheading yet again. Stuttgart to Frankfurt, Frankfurt to Vancouver, and finally Vancouver to Honolulu. I stared at the new itinerary like it was a cruel joke.

"Twenty-eight hours of travel?" I groaned aloud. But there was one silver lining.

A 32-hour layover in Waikiki.

That thought alone sparked a flicker of hope. Sun-kissed waves. The familiar lull of the Pacific. Maybe, just maybe, a few glorious hours surfing on a longboard under a pink sunset sky.

Premium class on the long haul helped, even if I had to shell out of pocket for a business upgrade out of Vancouver. They did reimburse it later, but at the time, it felt like a gamble.

I've been halfway around the world and back, across war zones, over oceans, into hotels and out of cockpits. But this might be the most grueling stretch of deadheading I've ever done.

Would Waikiki make it worth it? I didn't let myself get too excited. Experience has taught me better.

Because in this life, nothing is certain. Plans change. Flights get canceled. Layovers vanish. But if you don't hope, just a little, you start to forget why you keep going.

So I clung to the dream of waves, of salt on my skin and surfboard beneath my feet, and whispered to myself:

"Let's just get there first."

Chapter 28

Three Engines, a Coastline, and a Quiet Storm

In the midst of the chaos that defines this profession, schedules in flux, jetlag dragging like chains, and unexpected reroutes, I want to share a recent flight that left an imprint far deeper than usual.

It started in Lima, Peru. A beautiful city with a coastline that wraps itself around the Pacific like an old sailor's arm around a compass. But for us, there wasn't enough time to admire the view. We were loaded to the brim, carrying 107 tons of fresh, delicate berries bound for Miami. The cargo bay held a fragile heartbeat, produce whose value faded with each passing hour. We were at our maximum allowable takeoff weight for that airport. Every calculation had been triple-checked. There was no room for error.

As we climbed through 6,000 feet toward our assigned cruising altitude of 28,000, my eyes swept across the engine displays. Then, a flicker. Engine Number 4's EGT gauge nudged into the amber band.

I leaned forward, a familiar tension pressing into my chest. "You seeing that, too?" I asked quietly.

The First Officer, who was flying, glanced over. "Yeah. Number 4's EGT's creeping up."

I said to the first officer, "You have the aircraft", and I reached for the throttle, easing it back slightly. No alarms, no exceedance yet. Just flirting with the limits. I held it there, gently nursing the engine back below the amber range. A single exceedance would trigger a memory checklist, potentially escalating everything. I didn't want to go down that road unless absolutely necessary.

We continued to climb. The engine, though temperamental, was still producing thrust. I kept my eyes locked on the panel. Oil pressure, temperature, fuel flow, N1, N2, all green. Only the EGT remained edgy, but manageable.

At 28,000 feet, just as we were leveling off, the calm fractured. The message blinked across the EICAS screen. Number 4 engine failure.

"Engine 4 failure," I said flatly, my tone shifting to command. "I have the checklist, you continue to fly, I said to the first officer.

The cockpit, always humming with a quiet electricity, now sharpened into crystal-clear purpose. Aviate. Navigate. Communicate.

I brought up the engine failure message on the EICAS while the First Officer stabilized the aircraft. Our second captain, Cesar, locked in with focus. We all moved like cogs in a well-oiled machine.

"Confirming engine fail Number 4," I said. "Opening FMC cruise page… selecting Engine Out."

The Flight Management Computer recalculated its three-engine optimum and maximum altitude. It knew we were now flying on three engines and gave us a new maximum engine-out altitude. Luckily, FL280 was well within the safe envelope for our situation. Meanwhile, the First Officer applied appropriate rudder trim to balance the asymmetrical thrust.

Then came the call.

"Pan Pan, Pan Pan, Pan Pan," I declared to ATC, keeping my voice steady. "We have an engine failure. Request to maintain FL280 and requesting coastal vectors to remain clear of high terrain."

"Roger that," came the controller's reply, calm and clinical. "Maintain FL280. You are cleared for routing along the coastline."

I exhaled slowly, grateful. High terrain in the Andes could be unforgiving, especially when operating on reduced power.

Following the checklist in the book, I called for the engine restart attempt. No fire. No exceedances. No abnormal vibration. The N1 still showed rotation, so we gave it a try. But the engine didn't so much as twitch. No spin-up. No life.

"We're shutting it down," I confirmed. "Checklist complete."

While I managed the flight deck, I asked Captain Cesar to notify the company via Satcom. A moment later, he turned, headset still on.

"They're instructing us to continue to Miami."

I nodded slowly. "Of course they are." I already knew why.

Berries. 107 tons of precious, perishable berries. The clock was ticking, and the market window was narrow. Time wasn't just money, it was everything.

Now, for the record, let me be clear about the decision I made. FAA and company regulations are specific. In the event of an engine failure, the captain must divert to the nearest suitable airport, unless the aircraft has more than two engines. On a Boeing 747, a three-engine operation isn't that abnormal. We train for it. We know its limitations and capabilities.

FL280 was optimal for single-engine-out cruise according to the FMC. There was no fire. No separation. No critical system failures. We weren't in a severe emergency. That's why I declared Pan Pan, not Mayday. That's why I accepted the company's direction to proceed to Miami.

Still, we had to burn off fuel. Our landing weight had to drop below 295 tons. Otherwise, we'd be forced to hold and jettison fuel, which meant more checklists and more risk.

We followed our revised route northbound along the spine of the continent, hugging the Peruvian coastline, then

Ecuador, Colombia, abeam Panama City, Barranquilla, past Santo Domingo, and finally toward Florida.

Five hours passed. Uneventful. Almost serene, if not for the quiet vigilance that always lives in your chest during an engine-out operation.

As we began our approach into Miami, with the ideal fuel load reduced to below the maximum landing weight of 295 tons, the weather played nice. Clear skies. Good visibility. I let the First Officer fly the approach. This way, I could monitor, manage, and direct the operation.

"You've got this," I told him. "But remember, you'll need rudder input. If we end up doing a missed approach, it's your rudder, don't rely on the plane to do it for you."

He nodded, composed. We had trained for this in the simulator every six months. But nothing ever plays out exactly like training.

As we turned base, Miami Approach cleared us for ILS Runway 09. "Intercept heading zero six zero."

The aircraft, under autopilot, began the turn but never captured the localizer.

"Still drifting," I muttered. "It's not intercepting."

The aircraft turned parallel to the localizer, likely because of the asymmetric thrust. I requested a new intercept heading.

"Cancel approach," said ATC. "Execute missed approach. Climb and maintain three thousand feet and turn to heading 180 degrees."

The First Officer hit go-around mode. The aircraft surged up, nose pitching to 15 degrees. The autothrottles selected the maximum go-around thrust. Almost at the same time, I focused on flaps 20, positive rate, and gear up. Then I looked up at the instruments and noticed something abnormal. The aircraft began banking hard, past 30 degrees to the right. Insufficient rudder, I realized. "Too much asymmetric thrust, you need more left rudder."

I could not chance it, so I took control of the aircraft. "I have control," I said firmly.

I took over, pressed hard on the left rudder, disconnected the autopilot, and leveled the wings. Back to heading 180, holding 3,000 feet. Then called for the flaps to be retracted to 10 and then 5 degrees.

Seconds later, ATC gave us A 270-degree heading to a downwind leg for another try.

I was just about to re-engage the autopilot when, all of a sudden, caution lights, warnings, and flags showed up on my instruments. It called for a memory action checklist.

Airspeed Unreliable. Autopilot and autothrottle disconnected, I maintained wings level and held my altitude and airspeed.

I looked at my EFIS screens. My PFD primary flight display, which integrates an attitude indicator, altitude, and airspeed indicators, had gone haywire.

I glanced at the First Officer's side and compared it to the standby attitude indicator. The correct indications were on the first officer's side.

So I decided to hand him the controls again.

Your side is correct, so "You have control."

He took over. The glitch resolved in under two minutes, but I let him continue flying in case my side would go haywire again. We were now in night visual conditions, and the airport was in sight.

"Good to go?" I asked him.

"Yeah," he said, eyes focused. "I've got it."

This time, he flew it like a textbook. Gear down, flaps 25, centered, and steady. Landing checklist complete, we were cleared to land.

We touched down smoothly, rolling to a slow taxi. I took over for the ground taxi movement. It had been a tense, controlled ordeal, but we brought her home. 'It had felt like a simulator session, a recurrent loft periodic training that we do every six months. But it had all been real.

Later, the engineer confirmed it. Engine Number 4 had known issues. Reported before. Still legally within limits. They kept flying it. Until it failed. On us.

The Boeing 747-400s are aging. Noble beasts, but more prone now to these mechanical sighs and stumbles.

I filed the report in the tech logbook, then we headed through customs. I was running on fumes. We stood outside, waiting for our Uber to the hotel, when my phone rang.

Duty Manager. Then Maintenance Control.

"We need a more precise description in the technical logbook, Captain. Can you return to the aircraft to write more details into the logbook?"

I looked back. "We've already cleared customs," I said, politely but firmly. "They won't let us reenter the secure area."

I offered to wait at the hotel reception so the engineer could bring the book to me. But even then, despite my patience, my courtesy, my exhaustion, I was later reported as uncooperative and rude.

Why? Likely because someone in maintenance wanted to shift the blame. A scapegoat is easier to find than accountability.

There's always someone ready to throw you under the bus to protect their department.

But I had done everything right. And more importantly, everyone had landed safely.

That, above all, is the only report that truly matters.

Chapter 29

Biscuits, Blame, and the Eye of the Storm

The next morning, the hum of uncertainty rode with me on the train from Miami to Orlando. My flights had been suddenly canceled, my schedule wiped clean. The company had summoned me for a meeting. A tea and biscuit affair, they called it. That quaint phrase almost made it sound pleasant.

But I knew better.

It wasn't the tea I was worried about. It was the taste of what was coming. I had some explaining to do.

The meeting room was neutral and air-conditioned, tucked inside the Orlando operations center. My chief pilot greeted me with a practiced smile, his tone polite, even gentle.

"Let's talk," he said, gesturing toward a chair. "I just want to hear your side."

His demeanor was warm, fair. But seated across the table was the maintenance control person, and beside him, our director. The maintenance controller didn't say a word. He wouldn't even look me in the eye. That said, more than enough.

The first blow landed quietly.

"You've been reported," my chief pilot began, "for being rude and uncooperative during post-flight procedures."

I held his gaze, steady but calm.

"That's not true," I said, voice even. "That's a dramatized and exaggerated accusation. A complete distortion of the facts."

I explained, with as much composure as I could muster, that my demeanor on the phone had been neutral, perhaps fatigued, but never rude. After all, I had just dealt with an engine failure, the long, stressful night flight that followed, a three-engine missed approach, and a critical failure of my instruments, prompting a memory item related to the failure of my EFIS screen. I had saved the plane and the crew, and now they were accusing me of this.

"I cooperated with everything that was asked," I continued, " I spoke the truth when I told you I couldn't return to the aircraft after passing through U.S. Customs. That's not a company policy. That's federal law."

The maintenance manager, sitting stone-faced, attempted to shift the blame toward the engineer who had flown onboard. I didn't let it slide.

In front of him, I said pointedly, " I told you both, politely, that once we were outside and already in our Uber, we would proceed to the hotel as instructed. You suggested bringing the techlog to me, and I agreed."

And I did exactly that.

When I arrived at the hotel, I waited at reception just as promised. The engineer brought me the logbook. I documented the engine failure in greater detail, even though it was long past duty hours.

But deep down, I knew what this was.

The manager of the maintenance department had likely panicked. They knew that Engine Number 4 had been problematic before. They knew it had been kept in operation despite previous reports. And now, it had failed in flight.

Rather than risk scrutiny from the FAA, it was easier to paint me as uncooperative. To make noise elsewhere and divert attention from where it truly belonged.

Soon enough, the focus shifted.

The chief pilot appeared satisfied with my answers.

Now I had to deal with the FAA itself. The Safety Department wanted every detail. No cutting corners. The company reviewed my report and told me it was too brief. They asked me to expand on it.

Fine. I added more.

But I also knew my limits. I couldn't speculate on engine history or internal maintenance records. That was beyond my purview. I was worried, though. Concerned they might try to shift the entire fault onto me.

Would I become the fall guy?

Thankfully, after much back-and-forth, emails, edits, and clarification, the issue was eventually settled between the company and the FAA. No penalties. No reprimands. At least not for me.

That's life as a pilot.

There are factions in aviation that don't particularly like us. Jealousy. Resentment. Maybe even a bit of territorial hostility. When cracks show, some people are quick to exploit them, hoping to clip the wings of the pilot group.

After the dust settled, I was left in Orlando.

In limbo.

Four full days with no flights, no schedule, and nothing to do but wait. Hurricane Milton was closing in on Florida. Rumors buzzed around the operations center. A newly acquired B747 needed repositioning to Chicago. I was asked to stand by to ferry it out just before the storm hit.

I knew what that meant. The aircraft might not be fully certified. If it wasn't ready in time, I'd be stuck here while the hurricane made landfall. And I wasn't even on duty anymore. These were supposed to be my days off.

At the last moment, my chief pilot stepped in. He approved my release.

"Go home," he said. "You've done enough."

Later, I heard that the ferry flight had been canceled altogether. So in the end, I lost five days of work and income for a situation I had handled by the book.

Was it fair?

No.

But sometimes, in this job, you have to accept losing a few battles just to keep flying. To keep your reputation clean. To keep your dignity intact.

Of course, it wasn't over yet.

I still had to fill out an irregularity safety report due to the engine failure. Another round of forms. Another round of accountability.

But I did it. Because that's the job.

Chapter 30

Final Approach: Reflections of a Skybound Soul

The sun begins to set on my career, and I can already feel the warm breeze of Manzanillo Bay whispering my name. Retirement is no longer a distant concept. It's a sunrise just beyond the horizon, golden and full of promise. I picture myself barefoot on sun-kissed sand, a fishing rod in one hand, a surfboard leaning nearby, the salt air rich with memories and anticipation. Guitar melodies drifting on the wind, my grandson's laughter echoing in the background. Family close. Peace within.

I've lived a blessed life. If the end were to come suddenly, I'd go with a smile, knowing I drank deeply from the cup of experience. I'm thankful to god, to the universe, and to my parents for everything. The challenges, the serendipities, the loves, the heartbreaks, the camaraderie. I'm grateful for the health that carried me through the skies and the friendships forged in hangars and across continents. This life? It was never perfect. But it was real. And it was mine.

Life after 60 becomes simpler, however, there are three things that you never say no to.

1. A free drink,

2. An available bathroom, and

3.   A willing, loving female offering some love.

Would I do it all again? Absolutely. Maybe I'd take a different taxi route to avoid a few of the inevitable assholes. Because yes, they exist, and yes, they left their mark. But even those encounters were lessons wrapped in sandpaper. Sometimes it's friction that ignites the spark. No one evolves under glass. It's pressure, pain, even suffering, that forges better men and women. That's what life is. A crucible. And I wouldn't trade that for comfort or ease. As someone once said, "Easy times make weak men, and difficult times make stronger individuals."

As you read these words, I may already be somewhere in the South Pacific, wind in my sails, salt spray on my face. That sailboat isn't just a vessel. It's a dream deferred, now realized. A promise kept to myself.

To the next generation of aviators. No, operators of self-flying machines. My advice is simple. Don't do this for money or for the promise of jet-setting romance. The cash will disappoint, and the babes? Let's just say, have you seen the cabin crews on domestic flights lately? You know what I mean.

Aviation has changed. The glamour's gone. The long, exotic layovers have been replaced with short turns and cheap hotels. The days of classy passengers and wide-eyed flight attendants are over, buried beneath spreadsheets and corporate greed. Airlines are no longer run by airmen. They're ruled by lawyers and accountants, bean counters who wouldn't know a rudder from a rivet.

Modern aircraft, especially the plastic fantastic Airbus type, have become flying computers. Idiot-proof machines are designed to keep pilots as passengers in their own cockpits. The joystick? A glorified video game controller. The desk? More appropriate for paperwork than piloting. Sure, it makes the mediocre pilot feel skilled. But it makes real aviators feel mediocre.

At least Boeing still offers us the dignity of control. Cables and hydraulics, and even fly-by-wire technology, give you the feel of flight beneath your hands. When it counts, you fly the bird, not the silicon behind it. That's the way it should be.

But this is my farewell. A tip of the cap to a career that gave me the world. I lived in thirteen countries, learned five languages, and met people from every corner of the globe. Especially women, beautiful and unforgettable. And yet, in the same breath, I carry a weight. Missing two-thirds of my children's young lives. I wasn't there for many of their firsts, their falls, their triumphs. I was flying, working, to provide for them. It was a sacrifice made with love, and though it came at a cost, I'd make that same choice again.

We pilot's live on borrowed time. We trade birthdays for paychecks, family dinners for time zones. And often, it goes unseen. They sleep in, scroll through feeds, unaware that while they dream, we battle turbulence, fatigue, and time itself. This isn't bitterness. It's clarity.

So what wisdom can I offer the newcomers?

Start learning about dog behavior. Because soon, the cockpit will only need two beings. The pilot is to feed the dog, and the dog is to bite the pilot if he tries to touch anything.

Or better yet, get used to the idea of your co-pilot being a sexy, silicone-skinned Japanese AI doll. Who knows, it might be more responsive than some current FOs.

But seriously. If you have the fire, the hunger, the love for flight, for the smell of jet fuel in the morning, the math, the machines, the madness, then go all in. But don't kid yourself. This isn't a job for the woozies or weak-hearted. This is for the few, the mad, the airborne.

As an old captain friend once said to me, "The three qualities you need to be a true aviator are: love for alcohol, love for women, and love for math. Without those, you won't have what it takes."

He was joking, of course, well, kind of. Whether you stay flying puddle jumpers or chase the majors, just remember. It's changing fast. Soon, robots may replace us, and the skies will fall silent with the absence of real aviators.

We were the last of our kind. A dying breed.

However, I have lived to the fullest. I have survived cabin fires, near runway overrun, engine failure and bird strikes causing engine flameouts, TARA traffic collision avoidance, air traffic controller mistakes, nasty weather, severe turbulence, airport arrests, pissed off flight attendant aggression, the famous AIDS syndrome, meaning another aviation induced divorce syndrome, and did not get shot down while flying into war dangerous areas.

Why? Because someone had to do it. And I wasn't about letting life pass me by, full of adventure and action, making satisfaction.

I've had my run. My stories are now yours to read. Maybe they'll inspire the true dreamers. Maybe they'll repel the wrong ones. Either way, I've said my piece.

And if I offended you? Grow a spine. Life's not meant to be served easily. Stop blaming the world, or your parents, or your ex, or the universe for where you are. You're not entitled to a damn thing unless you earn it.

So, are you the lion or the mouse? You choose.

Now get off the couch. Quit smoking the ganja, it makes you slow and stupid. Get moving. Dream out loud. Print it, post it, pray on it. Make it real.

Visualize it and make it happen, using the law of attraction. Turning thoughts into matter. The power of visualization has worked for me; why shouldn't it work for you?

As for me, I'll be sipping a margarita on a hammock by the shore, watching the waves roll in and the bikinis walk by. Living the moment. Breathing it all in. Letting memories play like a slide show across my mind's sky.

And even when I am retired, while waking up every morning and something in my aging body hurts, it's a good sign because it means I am still alive.

And when that final curtain falls, I hope I get to say it with a grin and a wink.

Hasta la vista, baby.

Roger, over and out.

Sincerely,

Captain Enrique Henry Bligh Horta